Soul Journey

Soul Journey

A Write Edit Share Anthology

Dr. Manjusri Nair, Dani Glaeser, Kate Heartwright, Maria Kostalec, Kerri Beth Overington, Judith Loe, Heidi C. Tyler, Yvette Simpson, Smadar Asraf

Write Edit Share

Contents

Introduction

We came together – different continents, different dreams, and different journeys – with a single common thread. We began as Mindvalley Ambassadors for Lifebook. We loved our journey supporting others. We began as acquaintances, which became a deep dive friendship. We created a routine of weekly calls before the world pandemic created "normal" Zoom meetings. We became, grew, and supported each other through the joys of life as well as navigated losses in health and relationships. Sometimes that weekly call became a lifeline that we needed in that moment.

We created an experiment of writing as part of our weekly calls to enhance creativity. To grow in ways that we hadn't before. Nine strong women, who had already borne deep hurts in our lives, worked on finding a healing path to who we needed to be at our soul level to thrive. Soul Journey became a way of sharing something we created in the midst of turmoil. We stepped into the inner lighthouse of our soul. Each of us chose a word theme to write around in relation to where our journey focused at that point in time.

Now, it's time to explore our fictional stories, enjoy the journeys and your own Soul Journey.

The Legend of the Eclipsed Soul by Dr. Manjusri Nair

ॐ पूर्णमदः पूर्णमिदं पूर्णात्पुर्णमुदच्यतेपूर्णश्य पूर्णमादाय पूर्णमेवावशिष्यते ॥ॐ शान्तिः शान्तिः शान्तिः ॥

Om Puurnnam-Adah Puurnnam-Idam Puurnnaat-Purnnam-Udacyate Puurnnashya Puurnnam-Aadaaya Puurnnam-Eva-Avashissyate

||Om Shaantih Shaantih Shaantih ||

In essence:

Aum
That (macrocosm) is whole.
This (microcosm) is whole.
From that whole, this whole has proceeded.
Wholeness taken from Wholeness
Leaves behind only Wholeness.
Hence, Wholeness alone is.
Aum. Peace! Peace! Peace!
-Ishavasya Upanishad

This happened

The Shadow-knitters' Ministry was in an utter uproar. All the officials stampeded their way across to the Hall of Loom. Shadow-knitters covered the floor, the walls, and even the ceilings as they streamed their two-dimensional, grey selves inside. Slowly, news filtered in.

One of the Fates had sent the warp and weft of a Humortal's life weave all awry. It didn't do to blame the Office of the Fates since they did so obdurately refuse to take on more personnel. Every, albeit very infrequent, now and then, when one of them caused such a glitch, it took Source-sphere's entire set of departments and ministries thousands of years to smooth things over. Angry and confused, the Shadow-knitters, nevertheless, entered the Hall of Loom reverentially.

The Fates sat perched on their pouffies in the hallowed Hall, looking as youthful and inscrutable as ever. If it were up to them, One would shrug, Two would toss her head, and Three would wave the pests away. But they carried on with their graceful and delicate work of weaving destiny's fabric. Also, they didn't want the Source to visit them. Not now. Not because of a silly mishap. She would come down and look at them sadly. Above all, the Fates hated Her looking at them like that. Oh, they recognised emotional blackmail when they saw it. But you really don't want Her looking at you like that. Not when you've spent eternities ensuring that each Humortal remained connected to Her through the threads passing through Fates' fingers, painstakingly laying the holographic map for each S.O.U.L (Spark of Unified Love) to find its way back to Her.

The Karmic Administrator was beside himself because he

had a mutant Humortal on the verge of being born. He sneered at the monumental ego of the Fates. Spent eternities to make sure Humortals stay connected to Source. Ha. Destiny's fabric. Ha. Ha. If it were not for him and his team at Department of Karma Allocation (DoKA), there would be no continuity, no passages, no completion of the soul's journey. The Administrator stopped laughing. No one knew how this soul would make its way back to Wholeness, what paths she'd walk, what destinations she would reach. This was no laughing matter.

'Indeed not.'

All heads turned towards the voice coming through the Akashic Gates. One of the Originals entered the Hall, filling it with his mighty presence. Gaia and her beings were in his special charge, so he had the onerous responsibility of dealing with this mess.

'It is inconceivable to have a lost soul,' said he, 'A part of the Source-Mother, that may not return back to Her. The Source-sphere's very existence is so that She may revel in unlimited versions of Herself, allowing them free will, but always ensuring that they make their way back to her. I have requested The Grandmaster to –'

As if it were meant to be, The Portal of Eternities opened to reveal The Grandmaster of Time. He entered the Hall with his gears a-clicking, covered in the mists of time, springing the music of the spheres, while bringing his assistant, the Recordkeeper, along with him.

'Please standby as I halt the Flow.' Rumbled the Grandmaster of Time.

The gears stopped rotating, mists fell in folds, and music ceased. The Loom paused.

'Now, if we may know, how did this come to pass, and what may come to pass, hmm?' he enquired gently.

The Abbess of the Shadow-knitters Ministry responded humbly, yet crisply. 'As we're aware, all the concerned departments receive pertinent information about a new Life from The DoKA. This includes the karmic Document of Past Journeys from The Record Keeper and the Soul Imprint from the Source-sphere's Cosmic Intelligence Agency.

When the Fates weave the Soul's destiny, we simultaneously knit the corresponding Shadow-Self. In a well-orchestrated tandem, the knitted shadow, wrapped around the Universal Axial Spindle, is passed on to the Fates' hands.

Today, one Shadow-knitter felt a sharp and sudden tug which pulled the entire shadow in a fraction of the time usually allotted for a normal pull. Of course, we knew this to be a gross error, so we arrived here post-haste.'

All turned to look at Fate One. 'I hiccoughed', came the nonchalant response.

Somewhere in the Hall someone started making furious gobbling noises.

By now, the the three Fates had removed their hands from the Loom and were stretching themselves to loosen their bodies from a steady position at the looms. This was a welcome, though, unplanned respite. In the normal course of events, The Grandmaster of Time graced them regularly by pausing the Flow in between existential cycles, so that they could relax, take a break, and return to their task refreshed.

Since more was expected from her, Fate One sighed and

continued. 'So, my left shoulder jerked upwards allowing the shadow to enter the wrong rhythm of the weft leading to a tight warp of the Soul. The Soul is pure light from the Source-mother and nestles in the core of the body. The shadow is to be woven under the skin, but because of the tug, the shadow got knitted onto the Core-Light of the Soul itself. I'll stop here, so that we can process what that means.'

After several jaw-drops, eye-twitches, and muscle-tics, the following idea emerged: Fate One had misplaced a shadow inside the Humortal. The shadow-self had made its home inside one of Gaia's receptacle, the physical body. That meant this Humortal would not be able to cast her shadow. She had her outsides inside - literally.

Shadows are often ignored, but they play a crucial role in a soul's evolution. With Gaia receiving Sol's excessive harsh cosmic rays, Shadows protect the body. Shadows allow only optimal absorption of the rays to charge the core-light. This exercise calibrates the luminosity of the core-light. As the body grows, so does the ability of the core-light to absorb more of Sol's rays. A fully evolved Humortal is capable of shining by its own light. But this Humortal will be intolerant to daylight. Indeed, her very skin may burn and char. Most cruel of all, she won't shine on her own, unable to light up her life's path.

A Shadow is also the keeper of the Soul's dreams, desires, and lost pieces of self. These are cleansed, or reabsorbed, or disposed of, as per the Soul's free will.

Because this Shadow won't be able to execute these functions, the Humortal will often feel heavy of heart, fragmented, and unfulfilled. Without the illumination of the core-light, the Humortal will live under the pall of darkness.

With her Shadow covering her Soul, the map of her Self's past journeys would be obscured from her consciousness. Lastly, she'd be ostracised by her own kind for being a Shadowless Humortal.

The Karmic Administrator clutched his receding hairline, 'A Humortal without her shadow! We know what happens if a Humortal doesn't have a shadow, don't we? Well, no, we don't, because it's never with happened before by Fate One. Humortals have shadows, always did, always will. Just not this one.'

The Shadow-knitters shuddered at the thought. Thankfully it was a hiccough this time. That time, when Fate Two had sneezed! What a catastrophe!

One Shadow-knitter moaned and splattered himself flat on the ceiling. 'Medusssa', he whispered sibilantly.

Everyone in the Source-sphere knew of that 'drop-dead' anomalous gorgeous beauty who was way too much for Humortal males to handle thanks to Fate Two's sneeze. May Humortals be blessed for their love of myths and lore which blinded them to the cryptic and mystical aspects of their history. Perhaps the species deserved these jolts. Leave it to them to call themselves mere 'mortals' and distort the 'humor' out of their very appellation!

'To conclude', said the Original, 'this life may become, and remain a lost Soul, because her own Shadow has knitted itself around her Core-light. So, we have an eclipsed soul about to birth.'

The Fates' lips spasmed and the Grandmaster of Time looked grimmer – if that was possible. This was a cataclysm of hyper-cosmic proportions. There'd never been a case like this before. The Record-Keeper looked at the moaning Karmic

Administrator in commiseration. No matter who messed up in Source-sphere, poor DoKA always bore the brunt. For some reason, Karma had gotten such a bad rep on Gaia that everything from natural disasters to splinters in the foot was explained away by Humortals as, 'Oh! This is Karma!'

'Solutions, anyone?', rapped the Original.

Someone muttered, 'How about calling the Special Destiny Angels' Bureau?'

The room gasped as one. If there was one bureau the three Fates loathed, it was the Special Destiny Angels' Bureau (SDAB). It was practically a blood feud between the Office of the Fates and the SDAB, for obvious reasons. SDAB was the only department that had the power to veto Fates' decree. A low hum started from the base of all the Fates' throat. Sensing imminent danger, most exited the Hall immediately. Only the stalwarts and the foolish, who loved drama, remained.

'Call SDAB,' nodded the Original, 'and request them to send their most experienced Special Destiny Angel; one who has the power to call upon the seen and unseen forces of Gaia, especially the Elementals.'

After an intense dialogue with the SDAB, the Original announced, 'A mere Guardian Angel will not suffice for this case. Our most experienced SDA here will take over the physical form of the village Namekeeper immediately, and in time for the Humortal's birth. Being an elder, respected by all for her wisdom and abilities, the Namekeeper will be accepted as a guardian and a guide for this shadow-less soul by all. As to the latter's path of unfoldment, there's only one solution.'

He paused, as if weighing his words carefully, and then declared, 'She will be designated as Destiny's Child.'

Instant cacophony.

'This is a recipe for disaster, I tell you, disaster – '

'The Loom will have to be recalibrated.'

'All her previous records will vaporise.'

'The Record Keeper will be incapable of executing the probability calculations of her existential impact.'

'She will only have her own innate desire to come back to Source to guide her, if at all.'

'An eclipsed soul to be a Destiny's Child! Was there ever such a creature?'

Only the Grandmaster remained quiet in the babble until slowly all fell silent. With a gentle nod to the Original, he put the gears of Flow in motion again. Everyone in the Hall of Loom turned their gaze towards the village at the foothills of the unnamed youngest mountains on Gaia. Then, the Original, named Atlas, ever so slightly, shrugged.

Then

'It seemed as if Gaia herself birthed that child. The very air around us had become still for a long while, as though time itself had stopped flowing. Then suddenly we could feel Gaia's tremors, shuddering from her deepest core. They seemed to flow right through the mother's womb, who with a single mighty push, delivered the new babe.'

For the longest time ever, the *daimaa*[1] would narrate the story of the birth of 'that one,' to whoever was willing to listen to her rambling tales.

'While I tended to the mother, the babe was handed over to the eight elders to be cleaned and placed at her mother's breast.

She was a beautiful, bonny child with black curls and pink toes and tightly clenched fists.

The ninth elder, The Namekeeper, sat quietly in one corner with her scrolls, crystals, and shells. Over and over, she read her parchments, threw her shells, and counted on her fingers, frowning with fierce concentration. I had the strange fancy, that she was invigorated with newfound power. She seemed to have grown younger and more vibrant in those few surreal moments. I still remember, Sol was at his zenith in the sky when she finally made her proclamations.'

No matter who the audience, no matter how many times this tale was told, everyone would lean forward to hear *daimaa's* next words.

'This,' declared the Namekeeper, 'is an extraordinary life. Born to be called Tara, the star, she will be called Chaaya, the shadow! A mortal like us, she will not cast her shade under Sol. She will learn the mysterious ways of the night, and be the creator of her own destiny!'

So it came to pass Tara was called Chaaya. The simple minds and warm hearts of the village women made no sense of these words. They just knew she was theirs to protect and nurture. They drew their *palloos*², and set up the *uluru*³, heralding their determination to celebrate this life, even as the mother's tears flowed over her breast, mixing with her milk nourishing the babe's blood and sinew. She knew in her heart, that her daughter was an eclipsed soul carrying a great shadow within her, and that her journey would be long and arduous. Tara, a star born to shine, was destined to hide in the dark. She was grateful to the Namekeeper for having kept this a secret. Instead, the elder had done her best to imbue Chaaya's story with grandeur and glory. In times to come, the Namekeeper would be Chaaya's true mentor and ally against the vagaries of her fate.

During her early years, Chaaya was a happy and endearing child. However, she had to learn several painful lessons. Her skin had no protection against the blazing Sol. It would burn and blister at the slightest exposure. She was shunned as 'the accursed' because of it. Parents would not allow their children to play with her. She would often feel fatigued and revive only in the moonlit nights. Sometimes, her heart would feel so burdened, as if a great weight was pulling it down.

As if to compensate Chaaya for her many travails, the Namekeeper imparted a singular education to Chaaya. Under the protection of a mystical other-worldly grove, she was the only girl-child who learned the written word. She absorbed the language of the trees - Gaia's original 'World Wide Web', and listened to the stories of a mysterious place called the Source-sphere. She also learnt how to make salves for her skin, use dappled water to absorb more of the moonlight, and perform alchemical work with the five elements to cleanse her misplaced shadow.

> *My shadow lives in the shade that I offer*
> *It behoves me to keep my light shining on*
> *For when 'tis night and we merge as one*
> *I would like to embrace a de-lighted me in my dreams.*

Soon the trees, earth, wind and sky came to learn of her strange story. They spread tales of an eclipsed soul to the flowers, birds, coloured fish, and purple seashells around the world. Here was a magical child who could see with her skin, feel through her ears, and touch with her eyes. She was sure-footed in the dark, friends with those who roamed after sunset, and drank of the moonbeams to glow luminously herself.

She grew into a dusky beauty, lithe and soft-spoken, with a grave dignity about her, that kept taunts and insults at bay. If a few did reach her, she thought naught of them.

Over the years, she became a sought-after healer; her herbs and salves bringing succour to those in pain and sufferance. So Chaaya learned to carve her own path, protecting her own strangeness, reconciling with her fate. Her hut, the other-worldly grove with its mercurial lake, surrounded by lush forest and majestic mountains, and the teachings of the Namekeeper was Chaaya's universe. Her life was so much the richer and mysterious. If she yearned for more, making her heart grow heavy, she would cleanse her shadow and live her life as grace-fully as she could.

It helped to be awake under the soothing night-sky when silence had befallen, being amidst creatures who were at ease in the dark. It helped that night would blur all edges of separate-ness and do away with shadows, making Chaaya feel as if she belonged. Hence Chaaya lived more by the night-sky than by daylight. When young girls dreamed of their swains, Chaaya grew enchanted with the night, for it brought her many gifts.

Time and again, she would ask the Namekeeper about the Night. She listened raptly to the stories about one of the Primordials of Existence, who ruled over his Kingdom of Immortality and revered as the most powerful and fiercest of Gods, Lord of the Night, Kaalesh.

When others enjoyed the full moon and twinkling night lights, Chaaya would gaze into night itself. It seemed as if the light from her gaze would rebound from the depths of darkness and light up her own inner world. With closed eyes, she could see strange whorls within her and the play of light and shade at her core, as if she was an entire universe by herself. This then was her fated life, and Chaaya was fain to be left alone in it, revelling in her own thoughts:

Clouds could grow on trees
Who knew?
Perhaps dreams can crawl on knees
And reach the eye of a storm
Who knows?
And an ant can scale a mountain
To find a grain of sugar,
Did you know?
The ridges on my palm are encrypted stories
of enchanted lives
I have lived.
I know!

As is the way of the world, those who most wish for solitude become often hunted for sport. The village maidens and their youthful suitors, drunk on their vim and vigour, anticipating the pleasures of wedding nights and ardor of married life, took special notice of Chaaya. She had no suitors, this strange, shadow-less lass. And if there were a few discerning young men, they were quickly shushed by their aunts and mothers.

So 'Who would Chaaya marry?' became a merry ditty in the village. Having avoided her for most of her life, they cast their cruel spotlight on her, following her morn and eve, taunting, and teasing her. One night, they followed her into her grove, surrounding her, throwing soft flowers and sharp words at her.

'Where is your garland, Chaaya? Who is your suitor, Chaaya? When will he come for you, Chaaya?'

Backed against a grand old Banyan tree, Chaaya stated quietly, *'I shall be the bride of Lord of Night, Kaalesh.'*

'Oh, will you indeed, you freak? Naturally. Who else but the Master of nightmares and monsters for you? Will he be here for your *swayamvara⁴* ? Will he accept you forever? Or will he discard you in the bowels of darkness?'

Not for a moment did they believe her; not for a moment did Chaaya doubt Him. Perhaps that's why when she uttered those words with deep gravitas it impregnated a potent moment of time, reverberating with the creative hum that organises all the forces of the universe. Humortals know not the power of a clear pledge that can pierce everything, from tiniest of atoms to largest of celestial spheres. They know not that light particles and sound waves radiate thought and word to the very edges of creation- as they did now, whispering, 'Thus sang the Destiny's Child:

If I were to tell you of mine and me
Small and trite you might think
But my days were dark and my nights were lit with thee.
If I were to tell you of what I lost and found
I keep accounts you might slander
But all had meaning; mundane and most profound.
If I were to tell you of hurts and hearts
I romanticize, you may scoff

But I treasure them all
Each flower and the thorns as darts.
If I were to tell you of stops and ways
I wander, I'm lost, you may sigh.
But each breath and all steps
Led me here, in the now, in the always.
I know not the mysteries of you, O my Night
I know not the wisdom of my trials
I know that I have lived and loved,
Fallen and risen, given up and given you...my all.
I'm still here, I'm still walking
Nay, you may say, dancing
I know not to be an ingrate,
Life, I am.
Onwards shall I flow
Laying my own path
Seeding my own garden
Delighting in all that is you
All that is me
All that is us.

The Night was amused. So, they thought he was to take a bride, was he? He? One of the three Primordials, who was so feared by Humortals, they slept to avoid him. For alien they found what he showed them, especially what was within themselves. He would always show them what their eyes could not see, but they chose slumber, missing out on the wonders of their own selves and of Night's pageantry. It was left to insects, and owls and other nightly creatures to enjoy the spectacle he put up after each sunset. Oh, there were the sky-watchers, but they valued him for the paltry lights embedded in his Self. Him, they ignored.

Knowing the ways of Humortals, Kaalesh scorned the existence of the shadow-less bride, but news of her kept reaching his ears.

'The entire universe is suddenly one big broadcasting station,' he scowled.

Yesterday, she prepared her trousseau. Today, she beads the garland for Him. She creates a bridal tent in her mystical grove. Then she'd bathed with turmeric paste and washed with rose water. Later she'd adorned her hands and feet with passion-red *alta*[5]. Wearing her golden white and red silk saree, anklets on her feet, bangles on her wrists, nose-ring dangling next to her pink lips, she waited the next day during Sol's searing arc across the sky, for her bridegroom to arrive and claim her as his.

Even Night's minions started muttering about calling upon the Celestial Architect to build a palace for his Consort, sending invitations for a grand banquet, and preparing an entourage for the new bride. A hardy troupe of his attendants dared to ask him about his plans, and he responded with perfect courtesy, in biting tones, that sent them ashen,

'I'll be setting off on my multiverse tour within the hour. Have my chariot ready.'

And that seemed that. A multiverse tour often lasted incalculable millennia, bookended by varied types of armageddons. If anyone thought that the great Kaalesh was running away, they kept their ideas to themselves.

On the day of the *swayamvara*, all maidens and their proud parents gathered in the village courtyard, which was decorated with *rangoli*[6], *diyas*[7]. A small podium was erected, on which sat the musicians and singers adding their zest to the revelry. One by one, blushing brides made their way to the *mandapam⁸*, bedecked in the silkiest of garments, adorned with fine jewellery, scented, and veiled.

One by one, young men stepped forward delightfully proud and accepted a token of their intended's love and respect: a garland made by the dainty fingers of their maidens. With every match, there was much joy and cheer. Soon the new families moved away for repast and a siesta. There was much to talk about by the elders as to the benefits of the matches, while the young couples were allowed their shy amorous foolishness under watchful eyes.

Chaaya stood quietly carrying a golden yellow and deep pink garland awaiting her groom to arrive. In spite of waiting under the *mandapam's* canopy, Sol's rays took their toll, raising a few blisters on her feet and arms. Still, she waited. Once darkness set in, she made her way towards her grove. The Namekeeper made to follow her, but Chaaya gently stopped her.

'*I knew he wouldn't come during Sol's hours. That's not how it works, you know. Now that Sol has handed over the reins to him, my Lord should come any moment.*'

'Oh Source-mother, may that child's words come true,' prayed the Namekeeper fervently.

The grove embraced Chaaya as always. She took a few deep breaths, then treated her blisters and used her elemental medicine to unburden her shadow. Oh God, had she felt the weight of the Great Mountains within her chest today! She didn't doubt, she didn't hope. She didn't think of her yesterdays or her tomorrows, when placing her garland at the roots of a tall tree. As she had trained herself to be, she was alright with what is. And if there was an errant thought of lost dreams, a deep exhalation did away with that.

It felt like a scant moment when she'd sought to lay her heavy head on the soft grass, that she was suddenly awoken by loud noises – drunken ones, by the sound of it. The sky had turned midnight blue, when a few inebriated lads and giggly girls came to the grove, and espied Chaaya.

'Ah there you are! We couldn't participate in your *swayam-vara*. So where is your lord, Chaaya? Now, who was it supposed to be, hmm? Where's your garland, Chaaya? Don't tell us he wouldn't accept you because your dowry lacks your shadow -- hyuk hyuk hic....'

Suddenly they froze, the young girls whimpered, and the little men faltered in their stride.

Later, they would say, he seemed to materialise from the darkness, the trees, the water, the mist. They couldn't see his full form clearly all at once. His silvery eyes with their heavy-lidded gaze emerged first from the surrounding inkiness. Then his lean and wiry self, radiating blue flames around his corded muscles came forth. His flowing hair locks whispered loudly enough to set off ripples in the air around them. Each step that he took towards them made trees sway and created vibrations in the lake. Around his neck lay a fresh and dewy golden and pink garland. Deliberately, he made his way to Chaaya's side. Thus, the entry of that fiercest and most powerful of Gods, Lord Kaalesh, arrived at the *swayamvara*, to claim his bride.

In the village, the wise elders had deemed that the young be-trothed couples ought to be given the opportunity to become better acquainted before the sacred rites of marriage took place a fortnight hence. The air was sweetly scented with plucked flowers and the nights teemed with hushed whispers. Each evening saw much celebration, with soulful music, lovelorn lyrics, and agile feet dancing to the rhythm of drumming beats.

Each night of the fortnight, back in the otherworldly grove, a pair of lovers met each night, marvelling at each other's existence and having absurd conversations.

'Tara, my sweet one...'

'*My name is Chaaya*'

'But you are Tara, Oh Effulgent One. Permit me to call you by the name that sings who you are, not what you were given.'

'*You may*,' came the shy response, and then with a furrowed brow.

The next evening came:

'*Last evening, what did you mean when you said that, we mortals belong to the sky? We've always been told that that we are Gaia's children!*'

'Where's Gaia?'

'*Here*' she said, tapping her feet.

'And where's the sky?'

'*Up there.*'

'And what my beloved is in between?' he asked amusedly.

'*Space?*'

'Mm-hmm. What is the quality of the sky?'

'*Space?*'

'So?'

'*You mean we are surrounded by space, by sky?!*' Chaaya exclaimed.

'But of course! You are on Gaia, but in the sky. What, pray, begins when the edges of Gaia end? There's no difference between the sky up there, and the space around you. Perhaps a little more gravity, and lots of oxygen. But you do see, don't you, that while you live on Gaia, you are of the Sky?'

Chaaya pauses, *'But there are no stars around us.'*

'Ah. Perhaps that's why you came to be, Tara, my brightest of all stars.'

'Oh.'

Another evening:

'I don't have a shadow.' stated Chaaya.

'You never need have one when you're with me. I always absorb shadows unto myself. I'm the keeper of shadows. Consider a shadow is a part of me; always with each creature of Gaia.'

'Still, I'm a freak.'

'You're sublime. Your shadow, that part of me, has always been in close embrace with the light of your core. We've always been one.'

'How is it that I could never see your monsters whenever I was with you?' Chaaya asked.

'Are you sure I have monsters in my army?'

'So why is everyone so terrified of you?'

'They are scared of what their mind shows them in the dark. So, they close their eyelids and prefer to sleep. You, who kept awake, you who kept your eyes open, you could see in the dark, could you not? And you saw the truth. There are no demons or ogres in the night, save those that people harbour in their hearts and thoughts. Come the night, they can no longer distract themselves using Sol's light. Only those awake in the night can recognise their sky-selves. Those who worship Sol get seduced by his dazzle and remain tethered to Gaia. Only those who remain awake learn to fly. Indeed, mortals are blind to their own nature. If only they would open their eyes in the night, they would know that they're a potent and magical mixture of stardust and soil and life!'

'*As I do!*'

'As you do.'

'*I am Tara, the effulgent one, seer of the dark, born of Gaia, but a pure sky-self!*'

'And my bride.'

'*Why?*'

'Why?'

'*I chose you; you are my all. But how did you come to choose me?*'

'You chose me. Only me. Always me. You are the only one. You need not have done so. You could have yearned for the flickers of Sol like all others. All else forswear me, fear me. But you chose me. You see me. And, so, my bride, I'm yours.'

It was the best kind of romance, of two tragic lovers; one who had never opened her heart to another, and the other who had closed his to all.

Of course, news about the miraculous match made of the heavens spread, bringing envy and bitterness, carried by snide whispers and brazen accusations.

'We were drunk. How could we see Lord Kaalesh? Who knows with whom Chaaya carries out her nightly trysts? Why should we enter that benighted space? Ask the great Lord Kaalesh to show himself to the elders of our village in the morn. He must pay obeisance to our customs and rituals. Call him. Bring him. Or accept that you lie!'

Chaaya didn't ask for herself. She only wanted everyone

to see him in all his glory. She wished all to acknowledge his greatness. So, she asked of him the one request he could not grant her.

How to be by her side when Sol shone his rays? Why must she heed nasty words? Couldn't she understand how it smote him - this one weakness of his - born of Nature's rules?

A man in love, feeling powerless, can be daft indeed.

Hence.

'Should I cause an eclipse, dear Tara? Shall I bring ruin to Nature's laws for the sake of your petty neighbours? Shall I create a shadow for Sol to rival one that covers your soul-light, O my bride? There could've been another way. In fact, the only way, I can come and stand by your side during a morn is by standing in your shade. If only you had a shadow, my love!'

An impossible response to an impossible request. How it hurt! Her shadow within grew heavy with each breath, scarring each beat of her heart, she turned and walked away in quiet dignity. He made haste to follow her, but too late! Dawn had arrived, scattering his words in the ether, never to be recalled. So, he retreated, furious with himself, waiting impatiently to meet his Tara again the following night. But that was not to be.

Tara did not return to her hut that morning. As she was walking towards it, with his words pounding through her mind, which amplified all the insults and suffering she'd borne all her life, her heart caught fire. She made her way to the village's centre courtyard and sat under Sol's rays, defenceless and bare.

And she raged.

Intense in her anger, fiery in her demeanour, Tara, the

effulgent one, sat still under harsh light, with blisters forming on her skin, peeling off its layers, swelling her face. Tearless, blazing with the fire within her heart, Tara, the eclipsed soul, burned. No one could approach her, such was the heat she radiated.

Day and night, Tara, Destiny's Child, razed her own self. If the Namekeeper attempted to lather her with soothing herbs and salves, Tara did not flinch. If Kaalesh came to her after dusk-fall, she did not heed. If abashed villagers gathered around her, she did not see.

She remained ablaze, a silent scream gathering force within her. She flamed with her own resolve, shimmering the air-waves around her. Such was her intensity that the mountains gathered grey clouds to protect her. Sol agreed to be covered by a distraught Kaalesh, as much as was possible, without harming the children of Gaia. But Tara did not move. Winds froze, rivers boiled over, men and women cowered as Tara's power crested over the Great Mountains making them glow like molten lava.

For nine days and nine nights, did Tara burn red-hot, her fury welling up inside her, her slim body caked with burnt eschar, turning her into a living burning effigy.

Building to a crescendo, on the ninth night, she released a mighty, terrifying, roar, lasting all the dark hours, wailing from her scorched mouth. Its sheer force ripped away her shadow from her luminous core.

Slowly, her shadow spread itself in its rightful place under her skin, protecting her from Sol's light and carrying within itself all of Tara's dreams and heart-wounds. Having cast out her own shadow, unburdened and at peace, Tara sat at ease;

beautiful and sacred, having banished the eclipse from within her, fulfilling her self-scripted destiny.

Jigsaw pieces of me
of reality and shade.
Lost a piece here, a piece there
In the past, in my silences, in the rabble.
A holographic piece at a time
Fitting them just so
To form me
With a shadow that unburdened
In the sacred fire.
A saga of losing and reclaiming my Self.

A few days hence, on a pitch-dark New Moon night, Tara walked to her grove, wanting a respite from her overnight popularity. Despite her return to normalcy, she yearned for the embrace of its cool air. As she descended in the limpid pond, luminous water, lit by Tara's iridescence, fanned out, imparting a surreal atmosphere to the whole space. When she emerged, she saw Kaalesh leaning against a tree, looking at her somberly.

He knew; they both did, that Tara was no longer the outcast who had to accept the fierce and terrifying Lord of the Night. She'd received proposals from handsome young men, rich heirs, and even a stately prince. So Kaalesh held out the yellow and pink garland, still fresh and bedewed from their shared love, wondering if she would take it back, thus breaking their troth, and thinking himself to be an ass of the first order, who deserved to be alone his whole immortal life.

'My Lord, as you'd requested, I've arranged for my dowry; one shadow, in whose shade you may stand.'

'I shall proudly stand by your side, for all of eternity. Only say that I'm forgiven.'

She looked at him deeply and nodded slowly.

'I'm glad this happened, else you may have doubted that I'd chosen you because no one else would have me. But you came to me and accepted me as I was. So, in complete freedom, I do choose you, again...as always.'

'Tara, beloved, I am so sorry...'

'Perhaps this was Fate's design after all; that you'd help me release myself from being an eclipsed soul.'

'You did that, Oh Lotus-eyed One, by your own resolve, your own power, your own light. Henceforth, you will be known as Tara, Goddess of Light. All the stars in the sky shall be named after you. Oh Devi! Your nine days and nights of magnificence shall be celebrated as the festival of feminine wholeness. You, who birthed yourself, shall ever be worshipped as the primordial Goddess, who reigns supreme in the Kingdom of Eternity. And as for Fate, remind me to tell you of what happened when she hiccoughed, my love!'

Hearing his words, Tara lit up with joy, casting her shadow by her own light. Kaalesh came and stood by her side, holding her in his tender embrace.

Teasingly she asked him, *'Are we to leave for your kingdom after our wedding eve? Tell me, my Lord, where it's one long night all the time, how are we to celebrate our wedding night therein? Forever?'*

Poor beleaguered Kaalesh! That fiercest and most powerful of the Gods, Lord of the Night, blushed.

Punishing him further, she asked, '*What about this shadow of mine which has no existence in your realms, my Lord? After so much anguish and tears, what is to happen to my Chaaya when I leave with you?*

Recovering himself, he said, 'Ah, as to that, my Luminous One, I have an idea. Were it not for your shadow, our story would not have been. Your Chaaya is as sacred as you. As a part of you and a sliver of me, she will remain here, complete and divine, loved and venerated by all for eons to come. She shall stand as testimony to your strength and our love.'

'*And I?*'

'You my beloved, shall come away with me, making your way back to the Source -of -all -that –is –and –is-not.'

We leave the lovers there, making their plans, whispering love-drunk nonsense, and return to the here and now.

Now

Perchance if you were to visit a sleepy little village nestled at the foothills of the Himalayas, you may come upon an ancient shrine of the village deity, Maa Chaayaprakasha Devi. Her name means 'light of the shadow.' She is ancient beyond our calendars, and scientists have long sought to understand her mysterious phenomena. Made of an obsidian material, secretly acknowledged to be of non- earthly origin, Maa Chaayaprakasha has the ability to absorb sunlight during the day, turning darker than black, whilst the nights see a lumi-nous light spreading from within her. She casts no shadow, yet sitting in her presence brings calm and soothes all.

It is said that the Devi is born of light and night, is the pro-tector of lovers, a crucible of feminine power, and the giver of the sweetest of dreams. Each year, the villagers hold a festival of nine days and nights, called the Devi Poornotsav – the festival of the whole-being-ness of the Devi.

The mystery of the Devi deepens when one reads a poem inscribed on the walls of the temple in ancient script.

Wanted to write poetry
Settled for prose
But must a story
Be only between those?
Can it not spring from life?
And come alive in breathy pages
May not the pages be years' long
Encompassing telling ages?
Were it not for my two eyes
That espied you when I was four
There wouldn't be these tales
Nor this particular lore.
It is neither here nor there that our story begins
It is not here nor now that it ends
It lies between the distance of two hearts
That knew not they had to be friends.
Like all good writers, let me begin: once
Like all good stories let it take us there
To the space beyond now and then
The field that we all share.
Each blade of grass shall be a shard
Clean from sunlight and dew
As a mirror's blade reflecting
Infinity's light in us, anew.

Must I face thee and thy wrath
With trembling lips and fingers?
I think not, now that terrors have passed
And you and your fragrance still lingers.
Allowing to flow with hiccoughs
Of doubts and fears
How alive I came
After a bout of raging tears.
Never shall I promise I know all of thee
Never shall I promise to be free
That'd mean to repudiate the bond
That exists forever betwixt you an' me.
So let there be this mist, this shade
Let memory's songs go a-fade
When all stories are written and gone
Ours will be retold, anon and anon.
There will no hero, no nemesis
No troubles, worries nor strife.
Pages and ages of fertile dreams
Spread across the meadows of life.
Into this palace of givens and forgivens
We shall invite thousands who seek.
The lost, the found
The strong, the meek.
You and I accept this forever
This is our secret troth
That words and silence are our pens and inks
Wither souls' solace we shall wrought.
Why so amused are you at my naivety?
And wonder whether you wrote me into existence or did I, you?

Why does this conundrum matter?
I am your Muse, and my Muse, you.
And now, 'tis time to write our story
Strange how this comes about
Blank pages, filled inkpot
And my heart, still salving each sore spot.
You laugh, you cry, and wonder why
I nourish with my life's blood, these scars
Aren't you my love, O Night (there! I've named thee)
So very proud as well, of your paltry twinkling stars?
So come! Wrap yourself around me and my hand
Seep through my fingers and ink blue
To pen our tale for all
Those hearts: loving, brave, and true.

Tara

No one knows who this poetess Tara was, or what was her connection with Maa Chaayaprakasha. Such history is long embedded and lost in the majestic mountains. So, when a curious child asked her mother about Tara's story as a bribe to fall asleep, she begins thus, 'The Shadow-knitters' Ministry was in an utter uproar...

1 - Daimaa : midwife

2 - Palloo : free flowing end of a saree or a shawl

3 - Uluru : a shrill, high-pitched vibratory sound made during auspicious occasions, especially associated with invoking a Goddess.

4 - Swayamvara : the ancient ritual, wherein a to-be-bride would choose a groom of her choice from her many suitors.

5 - Alta : red liquid ink used to make designs on womens' palms and soles and feet

6 - Rangoli – colourful and intricate designs made of colured powder or paste on floors and walls and thresholds on days of celebration

7 - Diya - lamp

8 - Mandapam – a raised podium or stage, often temporary, used for multiple purposes from conducting weddings to music and dance performances

Move Forward by Dani Glaeser

She raised her head up from the dirt, feeling the pain in her body, broken and bruised. Blood, at least she thought it was blood, was dripping down her face. She could feel the dirt caked through it, and could only imagine what she looked like. She knew what she felt like though. She laid her head back down, the pain searing through. She couldn't do this. She couldn't get up. Maybe, if she just let herself lay there, she would fade away, and the pain would fade away, into the earth, turning into compost for vegetation of some sort. She felt completely and utterly powerless. How did this happen?

She couldn't remember. Yet, here she was.

She lay there in the dirt, eyes closed, listening. It was quiet, so she assumed she was alone. She opened one eye to look around, until she could wipe off the other.

She was alone, somewhere in the wilderness, and thankfully in the shade of the hot sun, she was starting to feel on her feet. Sitting herself up, she managed to brush off her hands enough to wipe her face. She hoped the wounds wouldn't get infected, but there was nothing she could do about it now. Here she was, in the midst of the unknown, wounded and broken.

She discovered the shade was created by a tree, so she shifted to lean against it, while evaluating her body and the situation. Her body was bruised. Her clothes were intact. She was near the edge of a mountain. Did she fall? She couldn't remember.

She was bleeding from her head, but there wasn't a pool of blood. She felt it caked into her hair, so guessed perhaps it had coagulated enough to stop. As her face was still a bit sticky and wet, but wasn't dripping, she took that as a good sign. She lay her head against the tree, and breathed. Thankfully, that didn't hurt.

She breathed in again, and felt a small breeze, and watched the tree above her rustle. The leaves were green, and she remembered enough that it wasn't an evergreen. Her body rested against the trunk, and she continued to breathe. She had no clue what time it was, or where she was, and there appeared to be no one around. Which way to go? Should she stay where she was?

Closing her eyes, she listened. She thought she could hear water, or was she imagining it? She questioned EVERYTHING. Maybe she always did.

It was time to see if she could walk, but first to try to stand on her own. Tenderly, leaning on the tree for support, she tested her legs. Aside from a splitting headache, she could stand and walk. She was also thirsty, as it was getting hot. She closed her eyes to see if she could hear the water again.

Go for the water. It felt like a quiet whisper. She didn't want to move, she was at least safe for the moment here, why should she go? *Go for the water.*

Closing her eyes, she listened again, and began to walk to her right. The ground was more dust and dirt with smatterings of trees and vegetation in certain areas, and the looming mountain of stone to her right. Other areas were just dusty and dry. She couldn't figure out where she was, though it seemed familiar.

Her stomach rumbled, and she realized she needed food. Great. She was now hungry, and thirsty, completely lost in the unknown, with nothing but a whisper of "Go for the water" and the occasional tree here and there.

Onward she moved. She watched the sun shift across the sky. Did that mean it was moving to the West? Or was it the East? Damn. She should've paid more attention in school. She thought it was headed West, which meant that North was behind her, and South was?

Her head hurt. Her body was aching. She found a tree to sit under and lean against. She let her body be completely supported by the tree, laying her head back, and then she let the tears flow.

"I can't do this!"

She slammed her fists into the earth.

"It's too hard! I don't know where I am going. I'm not even sure of who I am! I can't do this."

She let the tears flow, followed by sobs of grief for a life she couldn't remember, for a future she didn't know if she would even live to see, and a present that was painful and uncomfortable. As she cried, she became aware of the trunk of the tree on her back. Through it all, the tree supported her. It held her, at least she imagined it did.

She shifted so that she could hug it, imagining that it was comforting her. She imagined if the tree was alive, how it would wrap its branches around her, and perhaps whisper to her, "There, there my sweet child. All will be okay. You are just lost, and will soon be found." The daydream comforted her, and brought her solace.

"I guess I'm now officially a tree hugger," she announced to the tree. This small interaction allowed her the courage to keep moving forward into the unknown, hoping and praying to find water. She stood up, brushed what she could off, thanked the tree, and began walking again.

Eventually, she noticed she could hear the water. At least, she thought it might be water. It started out like a low hum, and the closer she moved toward it, the louder it got. Was it a mighty river? A waterfall? Encouraged, she picked up her pace, and noticed the vegetation was starting to get a bit lusher in areas. As things got greener and the air shifted to even a bit cooler, she found what looked like a path in between trees. She followed it, listening to the water with hope in her heart. Her stomach grumbled again.

"I may not have food for you, but hopefully we will have something to drink." Talking out loud, even if it was to herself, made her feel more human in a way she didn't know how to explain. And, since she was alone, she didn't have to explain anything to anyone. So there.

It was when she could feel the cool mist, she really got excited. Water! She could see more green, and as she looked toward where the mist was coming from, she could see that there was indeed, a waterfall, cascading into a large pool of water that trickled off into a small river that wove off into the greenery. The water was clear around the edges. The pool seemed to be quite deep in some areas, and the bottom of it was mostly stone, not sand or soil as she expected. She had expected a large waterfall as well, and this one was about 12 feet tall, with a lot of water, and quite noisy. It seemed to be connected to the mountain.

She felt a desire to climb up, and see where it would lead, where it came from. Her stomach rumbled. Sighing, she dared to drink from the pool. It looked clear enough. She would have to take a chance, and go for it. The water was icy and cool, and felt good against her hot skin. Did she have a fever? Or was it from the heat of the sun? Did it matter? She focused on drinking. The water was cooling and the taste was almost sweet. She figured it was because she had never in her life drank straight from anything other than a faucet before.

Was faucet water sweet? She always thought water had no taste. Hmmm... The pool had a few smaller fish in it, and as much as she wanted to swim, she resisted. She did wash off her face, and wet her hair. She hesitated on washing her clothes, as she didn't know if they would dry in time before the sun set. At least her face and hands didn't feel so grimy. Where could she spend the night? Walking around, she was tempted to sleep on a stone. Some of the trees she could probably climb and sleep in. She had no clue what animals lived here, or would come to the pool, or if they would want to chomp on her. Could she make a fire?

Everything nearby was so wet from the mist, probably not. She would have to have faith again, she supposed. As the sun set, she found a tree that felt good to her, gave it a hug, and cuddled up against the trunk, imagining that it would hug her, as with the other. It brought her comfort as she drifted off to sleep.

Her dreams were vivid and many.

She dreamed she was a dancer in a town square, swirling

and laughing with people. Her arms wide, her heart open, and her face to the sky. Swirling, twirling, and whirling. Her body and spirit radiating joy and freedom. Everyone around her had vibrant colors of blues, oranges, reds, golds, greens, purples, and pinks. They had dresses that swirled out like beautiful flowers, or loose shirts that also spiraled out when you lifted your arms to the sky. So much joy. Her heart was overflowing with joy and gratitude.

Another dream, she was mourning the loss of her life partner, the one who made her better than she was alone. She scattered the ashes to the winds as she sobbed and cried, releasing all the pain, longing for the comforting arms of her lover about her, screaming guttural sounds to the sky as she released the pain from her heart and her gut. It hurt so bad. How could she go on with this loss? How could she continue to live? She wanted to throw herself from the cliff and join her lover in eternity.

Next, she found herself on a farm, celebrating the harvest, preparing the food for the feast, various vegetables and fruits of all colors, shapes, and sizes. She could smell the herbs and spices, and laughed with friends as they cooked and prepared for the feast. Vibrant table cloths donned the tables, and then the plates that were many. Everyone ate and laughed, giving thanks for the food before them, for the people around them, and for the opportunity to celebrate the blessings of the earth.

This next shift, she found herself on another cliff, and this time she was old and tired and sore. Her skin was wrinkly and her hair was long, stringy, and gray. She leaned on her staff as she looked over the green valley before her. This was a pivotal moment. Would she jump, and end it all? Would she continue forward, climbing to the top of the mountain as she desired? Would she turn back from where she came from? Chuckling to herself, she chose to move on. She wanted to see the view from the top, to see if the old hermit really lived there. She wanted to tell her grandchildren of her grand adventure to the peak. She picked a purple flower, placed it in her hair, and turned to walk onward to the top.

Another shift, and she stood looking down at the feet of a child. Bare feet, dusty and dirty. She wore a bright green dress, also a bit dusty, that danced in the wind. Watching her feet walk, she felt a childlike delight within her. The child's feet walked a dirty path to the shores of a small river. Delightedly, she heard herself giggle as she danced in the water, splashing, and playing. At one point she slipped, and went under, but as the current was not very fast, and the water not very deep, she pulled herself up, wet and dripping, and oh so happy, because now she was cool. She could hear her mother calling her, and when she found her, scolded her, but then hugged her so tightly, because she knew her child could have drowned, but didn't, and was still with her. And that meant more than being angry for not listening. Her mother scooped her into her arms, even though she was dripping wet and carried her home, where she bathed her, and kissed her, and gave thanks that her baby was found and alive. She fell asleep in her mother's arms. Safe, secure, and feeling peaceful.

She had more dreams that blurred together in realms of colors, swirling like the fabric in her first dream. It was her last dream that woke her from her slumber, bringing her back to her reality of the unknown.

In this dream, she was sleeping in a field of lavender, a fluffy dog beside her, almost as big as she was. He was warm and protective of her. And when he started to lick her face, she felt a sharp pain as she remembered her injury.

Opening her eyes, she found herself looking into the face of a dog, who was quite hairy, and indeed licking her face. She dared not move as she wasn't sure if he was actually tasting her, or genuinely concerned, or what really. Inside she was just a little terrified.

"Sati!!!! Saaa-tee!!! Where are you girl? Come to me!" A deep voice called out, and the dog perked its head up and barked twice. "There you are... oh... oh man, are you okay?" A bearded man with a hiking stick made his way over to her.

She could feel herself holding her breath. Was she safe? Was he safe?

"Oh man... you've got blood and dirt all over you." The man knelt before her. The dog snuggled up to her, which she began to appreciate, because it was cold and the sun was just starting to rise. He placed a backpack on the ground, and began rummaging through it. "Oh, you are awake. Can you talk? Are you okay?" He continued to search through his pack, pulling out an extra shirt, and some medical supplies.

She moved her tongue around, and blinked a few times, before finding her voice. "I'm... okay... I think. I..." Did she dare to tell this stranger what happened? She had no choice but to trust at this point. She had gotten this far, and had no clue how much farther she would go. If this was the end, so be it.

"I think I fell, but I'm not sure. I know I hit my head, and I'm bruised, but I don't know what happened."

He looked at her, with stern brown eyes. "Have you been

asleep long?" He pulled out a flashlight. "Can I check your pupils, please?"

She nodded, and heard his sigh of relief after shining the light in them. "Well, good news is, I don't think you have a concussion. Can you walk on your own?"

"Yes, I think so." Her stomach rumbled loudly, and Sati barked.

The man smiled, and began to search his pack. "I'm Greg. And you've met Sati. Here... drink some of this. Do you think you can handle some food?"

She smiled. Grateful for drink and food, anything to help quiet her very loud stomach noises. "I'd tell you who I am, but I don't know who I am right now."

He looked stern again. "Hmmm. Okay, so let's get some food in you, and see if you can walk. I can get you to my car, and we can get you to a proper hospital, and then figure out who you are."

At that moment, I felt a shift within viewing all before this moment as if I had been someone else. I knew I would be okay. I knew then, that whatever happened, I would and could handle it. I was stronger than I thought. Oh, what was that Winnie the Pooh quote about being braver than I believed, or something? It didn't matter.

As I drank and ate a bit of food, I leaned into my tree, and felt Sati's comforting presence upon me. In a way, this was like a new beginning. The opportunity to discover who I was really, without the weight of the past to get in the way.

Who was I? Who would I be? Maybe I get to decide from here on out. When it was time to go, I was able to take in the glory of the waterfall and its pool. I would return here, some-day, and maybe I would know who I was.

Greg offered his support, and I leaned on him with my left side, Sati by my right side. I was tired and sore, but so very open to possibilities. And so very, very grateful to still be alive.

***

In the midst of the brokenness
 in the midst of the pain
there is an opportunity
to move forward.
And in that space rests
the awareness
 the ability to listen
and move forward
The soft surrender of the past
the uncertainty of the future
embraces you in the present
as you move forward.
Let go.
Be present.
Be open.
Move forward.

Dreaming by Kate Heartwright

The pot on the stove sings its song of warmth and heat, and soon to be coffee. I stare out the window wondering about the dream, the premonition quality of it, from early this morning. Kitten is wrapping herself around my ankles reminding me it is time for her morning breakfast.

I need to write this dream down. The quality of this one alone tells me my intuition has once again come in a dream form rather than the feelings in my body. I look at my table of notes strewn about and books open. Much like my concern in my dream; however, paper notes help me organize my thoughts better and the books have archaic references needed for my research. The research that pulled me to this little town in the middle of nowhere. A welcome respite from the rest of the world and an ability to breathe and feel again.

The coffee still has moments to finish before I have its warmth in my hands. I spy the pad of paper and reach for the pen on the counter. The couch will be perfect in this moment of time to sit and write. Crossing under the arch to the front room, I pause for a moment before I write, asking for help to remember what I need and have the details reappear.

"You must have me confused with someone else." I blush as I meet his frank stare across the shelf. Blushing appears when I am discomforted more often than when I am enjoying life.

"No, I am certain that I have seen you before, and I am positive we have met..."

I look at him with a slight frown that creases my forehead. I frown a great deal. I have been told it is because I am curious and I do lots of puzzling. I live too much in my head at times and not enough in my heart. Yet, I am wary of opening my heart. By not listening to my intuition, I have hurt myself too many times. In this case, my intuition leans towards caution. I am learning that connecting to my intuition is what keeps me guided onto a better path.

My intuition flows from my beautiful, joyful, full of laughing bubbles, higher-self. It is who I am when I am not in this earth-bound body. She is who I always have been through time containing strength and is full of love to give and receive. The earthly experience that I am here for is full of challenges, which include relating to others and not hiding my intelligence for what it is. Although, that intelligence happens to be a full part of my firm connection to my intuition and even higher in my spiritual life. I live and love my spiritual life. It just makes it difficult to relate to others at times.

My finger is starting to tap with agitation against my leg. Luckily, he cannot see my finger tapping.

"I am positive we have not met. If we had, I would remember. I don't forget the people I have met." I can forget where I placed my glasses or my purse. Yet, I remember details that others let fade back into their memories as nothing more than smoke, which is all part of my "relating to others" problem. And before he says anything, I turn and feel the swish of my skirt around my ankles and begin to walk away. My intuition rejoices as the tightness in my shoulders and stomach relax.

"No, miss, I am certain we have met..." he trails off. I can hear him keeping pace with me on the other side of the shelf.

If I didn't need this book in my hand for my spiritual studies, I would walk faster and out into the crowded sidewalk where I am thankful it is a Farmer's market day.

Unfortunately, I am going to need to stop and talk to the shop keeper. My neighbors, and others in my little town where everyone knows everyone else, laughingly call me the local witch. I laugh about it as I use my spiritual studies to provide healing that isn't traditional. Sometimes living in a rural area means that I feel as if I am living a century ago, and yet, that is also a blessing. Many of the town residents have lived here for generations, and then there are a handful of us who have been drawn here. This man must be a visitor drawn to adventure in the woods, and perhaps I did know him before I left the city life that I detested, rare as it would be as I rarely forget people. My intuition says no.

Reaching the counter of our general store that contains the lending library, run by a wonderfully warm couple who have been here for a long time, I smile. "Thank you for ordering this book for me. It is perfect for what I need. What is the purchase price?"

"You aren't intending on just using it as a lending library book this time?"

Laughing, I respond, "No. This one I am keeping. At least for now. As much as I enjoy sharing my finds with everyone else here, I need this one for longer than normal. I may bring in another one from my shelf if this one is as thorough as I believe, and the other is a partial duplicate of information."

My book collection may rival the shelves here in the store plus some; I donate many of my discards and the store chooses whether to lend or sell them to others.

"Why don't I just put it on your account, and we can balance when you bring in the other book?"

"Thank you. That sounds beautiful." With another smile, I walk out the door and into the sunshine. Hearing the bell of the door, it reminds me of the man. Somehow, I need the man's presence to remove itself from my life. I send a quick appeal upward to my higher-self and spiritual helpers and ask for help.

Being closer to nature regularly has helped my being more in touch with myself. Before living here, I lost myself in the busy of the city and the pressures and demands that were coming with my steady salaried job. My decision to walk away and find my passion was one of the best decisions I made. It took remembering what I loved at 12 years old to be able to find it again, and then several years learning which ideas did not serve me and were not my truth.

"Miss.... please wait...."

I turn, and pause.

His persistence means I am going to deliver a verbal set down. My intuition says to pause. "I do not know you. And if we met in passing, it was years ago. I have no interest in talking to you."

"I know, if you just give me a chance...."

I can feel my patience disappear as if the slow steady build of the volcanic heat is ready to erupt. Will the ash from this eruption darken the light and allow the freezing ice to form again in my life? Just as I am wondering what removing this nuisance would take, my dragon slayer appears. At least in my mind, he is. Every time I seem to have a large, unsolvable issue, he appears and slays that dragon. He slides his arm around my waist in a comfortable manner, familiar and not at the same time. If I weren't engaged with my impatience at the moment, I would be asking why he feels familiar. My body relaxes into his warmth.

"Are you having difficulties, dear?" his warm voice caresses my hair as he looks down at me.

"This, um, gentleman, seems to think we know each other. I disagree."

I look at him with a raised eyebrow.

"Would you like me to do something about this?"

I sigh. "I am hoping that with you here, he will take no for an answer."

My dragon slayer looks over at him, and I can feel the energy building within him. A dragon slayer hiding in this town, and I know there is a story behind it that I don't know. He seems to be a challenge solver for everyone, who has a challenge that needs solving. It is as if he is drawn to a challenge – confident in who he is, and where he is in life, which also sometimes is all he needs to be to solve the challenge. Besides his appearance when I am in need, we rarely have talked.

My intuition seems to have laughter bubbling at my wondering about this familiarity, and not sharing answers. So be it. She and I will have a discussion later once I am back to my home.

"You do understand that the lady is not interested in your attention." Statement, not question. I feel the muscles in his arm against my back tighten as he decides to step into my challenge. And yet, he stands beside me, not in front of me or behind me, lending support, and there again is a familiarity that I cannot place. What matters though at this moment is the nuisance listens to the no. I really am aware that my intuition wants this man who is ignoring my "no" to be unaware of where I live. That disturbs me more than I care to admit.

"Who are you? And why do you care?"

I sigh more in agitation than anything else. "You are not listening to me when I say I am not interested. Now please leave me alone. Your attention is not wanted." I am not turning my head up to look at my dragon slayer's face. I can feel the energy radiating from him. I also have no desire to see what look is on his face either. My mind is imagining him looking like the proverbial sheriff from long ago ready to do a quick draw gun battle as if we still lived in the wild west saloon days. Or maybe he is an engaging battle knight in banged-up armor, combat engaged for need instead of ego driven, shiny and picture perfect on horseback who avoids battles.

My intuition is full of laughter at that thought as my outfit mirrors both periods containing long skirt history costumes.

After a few moments of weighted silence, the man turns and stalks off. I am uncertain he has completely disappeared, but my intuition has relaxed enough.

Stepping out of the safety of my dragon slayer's arm, I glance up. "Thank you. You seem to have a knack for showing up when I most need you." I smile as those words register for him. "I don't suppose you have angel wings hidden somehow that we mere mortals can't see?"

My dragon slayer smiles, his eyes showing the laughter even as he relaxes into a more natural stance for him. "No. No angel wings. Are you going to be okay?"

"I am not certain. He was so persistent that this part of me is *feeling like he is going to appear again when I least expect it. I am feeling a little unsettled and just, well....*"

I trail off. I am not certain how I feel. There is a fear there that I don't understand. Deep and I can't understand why. My intuition is being quiet at the moment. I wonder what I am going to ask my intuition even more so than why my dragon slayer feels so familiar.

"*Why don't I walk you home and make sure everything is okay there? He will avoid coming near you for the moment as we walk, and then I will also be there to ensure that everything is secure.*"

I hesitate. Why am I hesitating? One of those rules that are not always necessary is coming into my mental view.

I think about whether my living space is actually 'company' ready. Because in addition to having left all my notes strewn all over the table, and been in the middle of making tea. Do I remember closing my bedroom door halfway?

"*Yes, please. That would be nice. My house is not quite uncluttered at the moment; I was in the middle of researching when... well, they called to tell me my book was in. I dropped everything to get to the store to get it.*"

Now he is smiling fully, and I can feel the amusement building in him. "*Are you telling me a book was that important to you?*"

"*I did manage to change clothes before I walked out the door....*" *I mutter.*

"*Will you tell me why?*"

I pause, glancing up at him, tilting my head as I wonder if he is genuinely interested. "*The book holds...*"

Just as I am about to answer him, I lose the focus to

continue writing and the dream is gone. I blink in knowledge and with acceptance. Whatever else is going to happen at the end of the dream is not important if I have lost the focus.

My plan of learning to listen to my intuition is not going quite according to my envisioned plan.

It seems my intuition determined that I need to hear it subconsciously versus just within my waking hours. All the practical advice I find on websites, in books, and from my eight lovely friends in this little village provide me with insights as to how to listen to my intuition.

I have difficulty making the actions stick for long, as I want to bounce from one idea to the next with impatience.

Now I flow and take the dreams that come and understand that the concept is there. This time it is clear; I need to listen to my internal truth no matter how much it seems to go against counter wisdom. My intuition is my higher-self giving me a nudge in a direction that I might not consider. I do not always consciously pay attention to the light, bubbly feeling when something is good and a heavy-leaded feeling in my stomach when something isn't as good.

The safety of the dragon slayer in the dream also seems important. Uncertain as to the importance and yet as with all dreams, the main concepts are more important than details. Dream details can change and be fuzzy as my subconscious does not always make things clearly recognizable. I also wonder whether this particular dream is a true premonition that some-times appear.

My former life ended several years ago in the old pattern. I drifted for years, letting currents of the others' wants just take me where I drifted, and before I decided to steer my life to a more beneficial current. The changes happened in response to life occurrences. As in my dream, I knew that the decision I made to step onto this path or at least remove some pot-holes and side trips from my path became the better choice. Listening to my intuition became a key and a learning lesson. I also recognized that all the potholes and side trips from before happened as I blatantly ignored my intuition. My current goal became to build my intuition muscle into one that I rely upon to balance my mind. Knowledge without intuition is less useful; knowledge with intuition is able to advance and move mountains.

Since I stopped my dream at an interesting point, I notice that Kitten joined me as I wrote. I stretch and wander back to collect my coffee from the kitchen. With a slight movement, Kitten yawns from the blanket on the couch that she has shaped into a nest, one eye blinks open enough to see if I am moving from the couch or staying. Noticing the movement to the kitchen, Kitten jumps down on her soft padded feet and follows.

As I pour my coffee into the mug, I wonder whether I will see my dragon slayer today, whether my book will actually arrive today at the general store, and if I will meet with my friends during our tea and coffee time today. A day full of promise.

Memorare: A mini memoir, composed of nine incantations By Maria Kostelac

...Never was it known that anyone who fled to thy protection, implored thy help, or sought thy intercession was left unaided.
Inspired with this confidence, I fly to thee.

For Roko
"A bird doesn't sing because it has an answer,
it sings because it has a song."
– Maya Angelou

COMPASSION & HEALING
Incantation
Memorare, O piissima Virgo Maria, non esse auditum a saeculo, quemquam ad tua currentem praesidia, tua implorantem auxilia, tua petentem suffragia, esse derelictum. Ego tali

animatus confidentia, ad te, Virgo Virginum, Mater, curro, ad te venio, coram te gemens peccator assisto. Noli, Mater Verbi, verba mea despicere; sed audi propitia et exaudi.

Amen

The journey
To wholeness
Is paradox.
It surfaces
'unmistakably'
to Mind
as Mosaic.
Not so much
a Return
as it is
a Remembering

...

Of our:
origins
birth rite
bliss
belonging
breath
A journey
through
not
to.

FURY & FAITH

"Our days are shaped by the legacy of your unfaltering love and faith in us as women of this world. We miss you, Dad. We love you." - W,J,F

Shrouded in accomplishments, rage besieged me through the five years culminating in this reckoning. A journey to faith - marked by incinerating fury. Love seemed scor(n)ed by loss, and only absence remained to mourn over. No grave. No hollow nursery. No miscarriage. No divorce. No failed invitro. Only flaccid self-indictment and a sea of quizzical expressions.

Dad's surrender to his cancer (a 3-year battle) resuscitated my heart. I'd fought to keep him with me. But an insistence to be home overtook his tolerance for the indefinite. Fortnightly flights tempered the void of his obliterated voice and the irony of mom's hearing impairment.

It was in his death's wake I finally allowed the lessons of loss in. They raised a periscope over my journey. Though dad had never sung a note, he filled my life with music. His love for folk and country music echoed hardship his un-mothered four-year-old self appreciated as 'universal acknowledgement.' It held me to a deeper appreciation of wholeness, than loss might connote, and stirred in me a deeper recognition of life's molecular music:

Rhythm: It plays out in patterns. Stand too close, and you'll mistake it for chaos.

Song: It serves to sooth. Underestimate its significance, and be lost to this service.

Libretto: Leave story to bedsides alone, and know only their breath, not their hum.

Virtuosity: Deny skill its abundance, and be left to flounder in inadequacy.

Virtue: Refuse truth it's allegiance to beauty, and betray the imagination.

***

DISGUST & DISCERNMENT

"I've learned that you shouldn't go through life with a catcher's mitt on both hands; you need to be able to throw some things back." ~ Maya Angelou

TELEGRAM

Telegram & Comms Co.
Servicing most continents.

From:	To:	Processed:
Wren Vogl	J&F Vogl,	31 August 2013
Heathrow, LDN, UK	Johannesburg, ZA	Heathrow Airport

Mom & Dad. Stop. I'm fine. Stop. Not happy but fine. Stop. Trip to US West Coast proved a nightmare. Stop. He spent most of it not talking to me. Stop. Pretty sure he's involved with someone else. Stop. Don't ask. Stop. Yes it would have been much easier for him to cancel the trip. Stop. On my way home. Stop. Have gifts for the kids. Stop. Don't worry about me. Stop. Will chalk this one too! Stop. Love you both. Stop. M

Wren Vogl
Heathrow Airport, LDN, UK

Telegram image

The umpteenth disintegration of Wren's love life had a cumulative effect. Months passed in confusion about the grief she navigated.

"I just don't know, Carrey. I can only tell you cutting him off is a relief. So, this heaviness persisting in my chest is driving me crazy!!!"

"Maybe it's a lack of closure. Do you need to talk to him?"

"C, nothing has been more satisfying than to have met his impenetrable silence with mine. Our lives would have been filled with deafening Coventry. No. No closure needed here."

"Then what is it, Wren? You can't go on crying yourself to sleep and waking up at 4 a.m., in a blind rage, indefinitely."

"Carrey, you hardly need to point that out. I agree. ... I don't know.... Oh! Thank you... yes, mine's the cappuccino. No Sugar. Thank you."

"Well...?"

"Some days I have to thank him."

'You must be kidding, Wren… what the hell for…?"

"For a friend like you, C! I'd have never joined the running club and found such kinship and support as you've shown me, if I'd not been at a point of utter dislocation."

"Hahahahaha!! Yeah, OK. Well, then I owe him thanks too. But seriously, Wren… dig a bit deeper. What's the ongoing upset about?"

… Long pause… Coffee sips… Wren scrounging for sunglasses in handbag…

"I think I stopped wanting a family, C."

"What?!"

"Really. The desire. The idea. It left. Too many eddies oscillating through the wish. It's hollowed me out."

"Oh Wren… You're giving up on love?"

"No, Carrey. Not at all. Just recognising, for the first time, what part of that is gone."

***

PATIENCE & WONDER

Wren Vogl - Morning Pages | 14 March 2009

I'm not sure what happened at the trade show yesterday, but I think I met someone I'm supposed to know. Or someone I should already know. Like he's from a previous life or another reality. We're supposed to meet to discuss something to do with his studies. But I can't see that 'work' is the reason we're meeting up again. I suppose I can only wait and see. That aside, this week marks my one-year anniversary in Holland. I've celebrated utter joy and frustration here. It's a true experience of being wildly alive. The blessing of the family here, who've boarded me and cradled my craving for sojourn, have surpassed degrees of generosity I'd never dare request. Surrender of my apartment and my possessions has been a release, not loss. In maintaining that all through my 20's, I now wonder if I somehow traded it for something else, something I was supposed to be striving for at the time. I just can't see how it would have had to be a trade-off. ...No matter! I have work in NL, I'm studying Dutch at the University of Amsterdam, subscribed to a co-working space in the centre of the city's Herengracht, travelling internationally easily, holidaying in Portugal soon and habitually lunching with the masters at museums and Het Concertgebouw. The work in my field is changing quickly, I can feel IT moving into the boardroom from the basement.

After all the years I've spent teaching IT-management, I can see I might be busy for as many years teaching IT-governance. I need more than that now, though. Something with more traction - of greater service to society. We'll see. This world crisis is growing real roots, and nobody seems set to correct the flawed premises behind the (more and more automated) bubble-bust cycles we keep seeing since I left school. At least Obama was elected. But Holland has responded in paralysis. Truly. One project after another is suspended. Rhythmically. Each week stories of people caught in limbo bob to the surface of reality, forcing life into a wait-and-see mode. ...A self-fulfilling prophecy of stagnation. If this continues, I will have to return to South Africa. I can't risk becoming a financial burden to anyone here.

***

VALOUR & PROPHECY

"Disillusionment was not without gifts. In the years succeeding my release from betrayal's brier, the corporate diversion I'd paved proved an illusion. Per chance, I ran into the man, who had offered me my first corporate position, out dining with his parents. His mother, head librarian to the Performing Arts Library of my alma mater, had been a guardian to my song years.

"The spouse of a cherished family friend, who'd peopled my stage audiences, prophetically, yet ludicrously, had once announced, 'We'll one day work together!' His tech-sector profession bore little resemblance to my thespian credentials. A decade later I was teaching technology-consulting practices to peers, from the payroll of his firm.

"The medicine of these moments was to reveal the fractal-firehose of the soul's reach. It smudged the divide between the disinheritance I'd engineered from its pure-expression by sole-obsession: extinguishing reliance upon others. Connivingly my inner-protector had intended that those who might see fit to pull the rug - their own agenda had woven - from under my stride would be neutralised. She'd seemingly traded 'calling' for 'career', and I was at the mercy of a collar her convictions (of distrust) had secured around my heart.

"Gratefully, Life is kindly amused at our bumbling bustle against its currents of inevitability. I was to learn this by several more intercessions of benevolent coincidence, as both 'career' and consciousness to which I would awaken unfurled.

"A quiet confidence in 'the stream' secretly settled in my

cells, like fine sediment gathers aground, defying the busyness of surface flow. Courage was to be its sprout – something my youthful ambition knew nothing about."

Extract from "Inflections: A Memoire" by Wren Vogl

***

LEARNING & EARNING

Wren revelled in her luck at living the tide of a world diminishing in divides. Hers was a youth witness to the simultaneous crumble of Apartheid, Berlin's Wall, and The Soviet Union - propelled by the rise of the internet, mobile phones, electronic commerce, knowledge working, unprecedented interconnectivity, globalisation, access to information and a rampant desire for social-inclusivity.

Wren's one life-threshold after another was breached in a mere half-decade. She secured her first paying job (of many to come), matriculated, studied a theatre degree, navigated ruinous first-love, and graduated (twice).

Song charte(r)ed her course. Performance perforated her soul. From musical-leads, to one woman shows, a cappella groups, wedding serenades, funeral devotions, carolling and family scores... Wren's songs would have been forgiven for thinking they were responsible for the sun's dusk and the moon's dawn.

She had followed her calling and ridden waves of unfaltering enthusiasm, curiosity, love, exploration, and purpose. Heart, wide open, she sucked the world in whole. Each person and project entered her path, embraced by unedited affection.

Flushed with the innocence of pure desire and unbridled support, Wren's raw trust in the world attracted the kind of betrayal only naïve love (and success) can.

***

MIRTH & MIRACLES

'92

Dear Diary,

I could choose my own subjects this year. I opted for the humanities. The school finally opened up to all races. Only one new girl joined our year, of 250 odd. She seems lonely and scared. She's not in any of my classes. I hope she's okay. Big changes are ahead. The whole country voted overwhelmingly for mass reform in a referendum this year. Dad says we're lucky the country didn't sink into war.

'91

Dear Diary,

This is a tricky year. The white schools around the country opened up to all races. Our school is late changing to a new system because the parents elected to switch from fully state-subsidised to partially private and Mom says they are still figuring out how that works before all the new kids can come to the school. I'm doing my best to learn Zulu, but I don't think it really helps if I can only say words and not sentences.

'90

Dear Diary,

I have mixed feelings about high-school. The first 2-weeks

involved walking around in our classes (maintaining rows of alphabetical order) with a sign reading "My name is ...., and I'm a S.L.U.G." a.k.a. Silly Little Ugly Grunt. Aside from having to accessorise this sign with my metal-grin and the cutest guy in our class behind me all year, the bright side is 'I'm a girl.' Boys are taking more strain. We rehearsed evenings and weekends for the Standard 6 variety show. I was in 3 different pieces - for the French class's number, the drama club's skit, and the poetry-slam. It was nice getting to know the class, but I made Dad fetch me early the day of dress rehearsal, to watch Mandela's release. The week after the show was done, Oma died. Mom talks about her a lot still. I started singing lessons too.

'89

Dear Diary,

I can't wait to get out of primary school! Finally. The only thing that makes me sad to leave is that Juliette's not coming with me. Why she's chosen to go to the girls' school. I don't understand. I can't. Most of our friends are boys. I don't trust the girls, except J. They mostly take turns ganging up against each other. The boys are more focused on soccer - even though they say stupid things and get into fights. Dad says he's glad I know what I want, even though he has to drive less for the girls' school. He never moans about anything we want. He just likes to make it happen. Mom is happy too. But she's with Oma a lot now, since Oma had to go to the care home.

'88

Dear Diary,

I have a new friend. Juliette! We laugh a lot. And we make

a lot of stuff. Fimo figurines. Wood wells. She shrinks chip packets in the oven!! She's like another sister. Her folks are great too. They don't mind me visiting and they let J stay with us weekends too. I've spent most of this summer wrinkled up from being in the pool all day. We signed up to do library-duty together this autumn... Which is better than having to do that with someone you don't know. The only downside to the summer was getting braces, but Mom says I can be grateful because I have more teeth than my head can hold and we have to sort that out. Oma is staying with us now, but she doesn't know who I am anymore and she's starting not to recognise Mom some days too. Before she was just forgetting things she'd said or stories she'd told. But now she's forgetting us. She looks scared a lot. Dad always sorts things out. Even Oma stops being scared around him. The only time he looks concerned is when he watches the 7 o'clock news.

***

FROM FEAR, TO PIONEER

ACT I

THUMBS DOWN

Scene 1   At Wren's bedside   Bedtime

Scene 2   Overheard conversation, by Wren,
                       from kitchen after 'lights out'

ACT II

SCHOOL NURSE

Scene 1   Uninvited Guest   Noon

ACT III

SCHOOL PLAY

Scene 1   Brave Mouse   Evening

ACT I

THUMBS DOWN

SCENE 1

(Wren's bedroom, and bed, holds centre stage; with the passage and kitchen off stage-left. Mom kneels at Wren's bed-side; enquiring of her 5-year-old daughter how she comes to be so determined to stop sucking her thumb.)

MOM

Do you want your edgy?

WREN

No. It's ok, ma.

MOM

Schat, it's a lot to handle. Why don't you wait a while before you take this big step? Wren, no one needs to know...

WREN

No, ma. I promised dad. And he said I'll get bad teeth if I keep sucking my thumb, ma.

(Guilty pause.)

... I don't want bad teeth,

MOM

(Sighs deeply and pauses to take in the significance of what Wren's saying.)

I'll sing to you before you go sleep...? Would you like that...?

WREN

(Hesitates. Nods)

...Just stroke my head, ma.

MOM

Do you want the light on?

WREN

No. I like the dark.

MOM

(Sings "the White Horse Inn")

(Fade spotlight on Wren's bed as Wren nods off after 2 verses.)

SCENE 2

(Mom's footsteps sound rhythmically down the passage-way, behind Wren's room, and fade-out stage-left. Voices emerge over the sound system, as if we are 'Wren' hearing her parents' conversation from the household kitchen.)

MOM

Schat, she's just five, and so much is changing for her. We don't need to put more pressure on her right now. What's wrong with her going to sleep with her comforts?

DAD

When is it a good 'time', hon? Life is full of pressures and we don't want her developing bad habits we could have helped curb, before they cause her bigger problems than what they solved?

MOM

(Doubtful, but understanding of his thinking...)

I don't know, schat. You know she's had a difficult time adjusting to school from home, with both her sisters still here. Her teacher says she cries for us every morning. We need to reduce the pressures on her right now, not up the ante.

DAD

(nods his head knowingly...)

Mmmm... (nods)

ACT II
SCHOOL NURSE
SCENE 1

(Lights fade up onto centre-stage to reveal a cosy living room, arranged around a television-set of the early 80's. Mom enters carrying a tea tray with pot and scones. She is wearing her house coat, having just baked a batch of scones for morning tea with her girls.)

MOM

Girls!! Come drink tea. Scones are readyyyyyy!!!

(The sisters yell gleefully in the background while Mom places the tea-tray on the coffee table. Thumping footsteps overtake the background with voices of little girls shouting 'We're coming!' Mom loads the video machine and the introductory sounds of Mary Poppins fill the room.)

SISTER 1 – Jess (age 3)

(Rushing in to sit in front of the tea and scones with her doll, dressed in her pyjamas and fluffy nightgown.)

I'm here!

MOM

Wait for Fifi, Jess... Where's your colouring books?

(Mary Poppins' soundtrack plays in the background. Jess tucks into the food, ignoring instructions).

SISTER 2 – Fifi (age 2)

(Waddles in wearing matching night clothes with her fluffy toy, to join Jess at the tea-tray with her sippy-cup.)

(Doorbell rings. Mom walks over to the front-door, stage-right. Lighting cue, far-right, front-of-stage, as nurse is revealed- standing poised outside the front door, with clipboard and document folder. Mom opens the door.)

MOM

Yes? Hello... Can I help you?

NURSE

(Dressed in clinic nurse's uniform, the nurse extends a hand to shake Mom's.)

Mrs. Vogl, I'm from your daughter's school...

MOM

(Panicked interruption... hands to mouth and heart.)

Ohmigod!!! Is she alright?!

NURSE

(Retracts her hand and answers - immediately reassuring.)

Yes. Yes. She's perfectly safe. There's no need to worry. We've been asked to make a house-call because she's still crying each morning 30-minutes after school starts. It's been six-months since she started school this year. Her teacher felt we needed to discuss the situation with you, personally.

MOM

(Confused. But matter-of-fact.)

I don't understand. What's to discuss? She misses home.

NURSE

(Burying her clipboard in the carry case slung over her shoulder and peering pre-emptively into the house over Mom's shoulder)

May I come in?

MOM

(Taken aback, but coming to attention standing aside and showing her in.)

Of course. Please... Come in. Join us for tea and a scone?

NURSE

Thank you. Yes... that sounds wonderful.

(Stepping in as the background sounds of Mary Poppins amplify and the children giggle at antics on the screen.)

MOM

Let's talk at the dining table while the kids drink tea and colour in front of the movie. I promised the girls a tea-party and because it's been so cold, we're all still in night-clothes to snuggle under the covers with the movie.

(Mom takes the teapot and scones from the coffee-table and a couple of cups from the nearby sideboard. They sit down as Mom dishes out the treats.)

NURSE

(Smiling)

This is lovely. Thank you.

(Stirring her tea.)

(Fifi rushes up to her with a page covered with prolific scribbles in multicolours)

What's this?

FIFI

For you.

(Proudly handing her the paper ceremoniously, arm out-stretched.)

NURSE

(Beaming.)

Oh, my goodness, darling! Thank you! How beautiful! Did you do this all by yourself?

(Fifi nods.)

Can you show me who all these characters are? I love the smiling sunshine.

FIFI

(Pointing at the page full of unintelligible scribbles.)

That's mom, me, Jess, Wren, dad...

MOM

(Endeared, Mom picks Fifi up to her lap and grabs colouring pencils from the sideboard behind her. She's anxious to know why the nurse's visit is necessary.)

Please, sister... What brings you here? I need to understand.

(Seeing that Jess has jumped on the couch with the quilt, Fifi jumps off Mom's lap and waddles to the couch, climbing up to joining Jess under the covers with cushions, cuddling up and giggling at the screen antics again.)

NURSE

(Smiling at the scene unfurling in front of her, she jerks back to attention, hearing Mom's imploring tone.)

Mrs. Vogl. I must apologise. My presence here is a formality we can't avoid when a child reflects behaviours indicating some kind of trauma. I realise now, being here, that Wren is utterly fraught to being away from all of this. If I were her, I'd cry to go to school every day as well. I'm so sorry to have disturbed your morning. Please be peaceful that my feedback will reflect these sentiments.

(Finishes up her tea and packs up her things, readying to leave.)

MOM

(Relieved and relaxing.)

Please visit any time, if you're in the area. Things have moved so quickly since moving here and I haven't made nearly enough friends.

NURSE

I will. You're kind. Thank you.

(Hugs mom and picks up her things to leave)

(Lights fade to dark as the audio prompt for Act III fades in)

ACT III

SCHOOL PLAY

SCENE 1

(Later that year: The school play is staged to celebrate year-end. The proscenium-arch curtains are closed. A tinny voice-over, as if accidentally, from back-stage broadcasts Mom's loud, whispering voice, over the auditorium's live audience.)

MOM

Okay, Wren. You're up in a few moments. Let's check your tail is on securely.... Quietly... Right.... Turn around... let's check your ears are fastened... Okay... Here! Let me fix your make-up again. It's smudged. Don't touch your face. ...Here, wipe handies...? Good girl!! *MWAH!!*

(Canned applause rings out over the sound-system and the proscenium-curtain rises to reveal 5-year-old Wren in her grey mouse-costume (leotard) among a chorus-line of peers in like mouse-suits. On cue, children's voices fill the air, as Wren belts out the vocal score, marching to the lyrics of "I'm a Brave, Brave Mouse".)

I'm a brave, brave mouse.
I go marching through the house.
And I'm not afraid of anything.
For danger I'm prepared,
And I'm never, never scared.
No, I'm not afraid of anything.

What about a cat?..

(The rest of the song, and sound of the children's voices, fade out as the lights fade with it, and the curtain slowly falls.)

***

FIRST LOVE

*dmmdmmdmdmddmmmdmdmdmmmdmdmmddmd-
mdmmmdmdmdmmdmdmdmm*

My first, my last, my everything | A triple trimester dance-debut.

And the answer to all my dreams | Ma sings and dances. A lot.

You're my sun, my moon, my guiding star | Ma talks. A lot.

I know there's only, only one like you | Oma sews. A lot.

There's no way they could have made two | Da-da daaaaa-daaaaa Dad!

You're, you're all I'm living for, your love I'll keep forever-more | Jimmy?

You're the first, you're the last, my everything | The White Horse Inn, at the...

In you I've found so many things | ... there's joy the whole summer through

A love so new, only you could bring | There's sunshine ever in store there

Can't you see it's you? You make me feel this way | Happiness stands at the door there

You're like a fresh morning dew on a brand-new day | The days fly past

I see so many ways that I | I must leave at last

Can love you 'til the day I die | But still whatever we do

You're my reality, yet I'm lost in a dream | We'll hear when twilight is falling

You're the first, the last, my everything | The white horse is calling to you

I know there's only, only one like you | It's time.

There's no way they could have made two | No. Wait... It's not...

Girl, you're my reality, but I'm lost in a dream | Ugh...

You're the first, you're the last, my everything | So. Cold.

You and me baby | Told Your Mama Not to Worry

It's you, and me | Something about soh weh toh??

And you are the first, the last, my everything | Father's Day

The End Begins by Kerri Beth Overington

This is weird. Time standing still, perceptibly. Pause in the suspended space between moments. Between us. No one makes a move, no one questions why a room full of dozens of peers retreat into obscurity. The energy shifts to something I hadn't been aware could happen. It's languid here. No temperature, sound, thought. Peaceful familiarity.

In one confounding moment I am clear.

There's an introduction happening here. I'm oblivious for a brief moment, then back to reality. Standing in a new suit and shoes I had spent all my money on for the interview. I'd risked my shabby studio apartment with brown water running from the taps in hopes of getting this job. Turning my eyes away, I try to establish ground. Feeling uncomfortable and on display in my ivory skirt and heels, looking out over a sea of oneness. Shirts, ties, clean cut, phones in hand. Simultaneous voices in harmonic noise, hundreds of single eyes cast sideways upon me...fresh, meat. I was told these men are sharks. Hired to feed on opportunity. If they weren't, they would not be here doing this job.

I've been given clear instruction, 'They will all try. Do

not let them.' At this point in life, heeding advice is not my aptitude, in fact it's the driver's seat in a luxury sports car on an open road. It isn't intentional defiance that plants the seed. It's too many words in one sentence. I only hear an instructive: sharks, date them. The rest of the words are filler.

Open road, a fast car, and an inexperienced driver.

II

It's a first attempt but the butcher has walked me through the process. Tie, loop, twist, slide under, until the meat is bound. The Yorkshire was a good idea from Angela. Her recipe from back home results in a golden swell lifting high in the oven. It is his favourite, and tomorrow the leftovers are perfect refrigerator cold with a dollop of fresh strawberry jam. Nice touch. Strawberries arrive early here, juicy and saturated scarlet, a hot May sweetening. Berry compote on sponge with whipping cream from the local cows will please everyone tonight. I made the sponge cake with the cookbook and whisk I received the previous year for my birthday. Or was it two years ago? I guess it was.

The sun is lowering. Everything is bathed in light. Late spring's evening air cooling hints of summer. I glance in the mirror; long waves of auburn graze my shoulders then fall past. A pretty gown skims taut limbs. The house, the food, and everyone is ready. Assessing my surroundings - nothing has been missed. Crossing the room to the step of that catchy tune whispering in the background, my view spans across the glass house front. The guest of honour passes along the stone wall and turns up the path. He declined a ride, like he always does, preferring to walk, saunter. He used to tease that he could walk behind me all day mesmerized, but it's me who finds his rhythmic spiccato compelling. Young success presuming confidence.

One, two, three...four cars line the street under bright green explosions of new leaves. The birds never leave here in winter like they did in my childhood. The trees are dotted, optimism of trusting hatchlings rising over the melody in my head. I open the door and he steps inside to join us.

A wave ripples through the main floor as everyone arrives to greet him.

Looking up at him smiling, my nose and cheeks freckled after a day under a spotless sky. I slide the trench coat casually draped from his forearm. The British always expect a down-turn of weather. Walking into the warm glow of the sitting room, I place the coat onto a hanger and close the closet door.

The young men look fine in their clothes, taught to dress for any setting, conscious of the grace in which they move. Raised to have confidence and to be mindful of presenting themselves. Aware of their effect on others. A dying skill-set necessary for survival here. Laughter fills the living room. The magic and exuberant energy of the boys raise everyone's spirits, ensuring the limelight is always theirs in our circle. They engulf him and he concedes, reveling in mutual affection.

I leave them to it, slipping away unnoticed. Returning to the kitchen, the smell of dinner is knee buckling incredible. Thankfully. Lifting the roast from the pan, setting it on the platter to rest, my twining holds its dripping succulence. A spoonful of flour into the pan, the drippings simmer into a bubbling roux like my dad learned as a summer military cook.

Turning my back, I pick up two bowls. One with tender carrots, the other with the fluffy Yorkshires softening in their centers and carry them to the table. The dining room setting with tonight's celebration is exactly as imagined. I slip past the new walls coloured the fair and juicy inside of a pear. Soft green trim work blurring the separation between here and gardens beyond the glass. Botanic branching prints the room more of the same with additions of soft chestnut and flushes of lychee, whisper pink muting bold vermillion ripening. We spend hours here daily, sunrises stream above steaming buttery biscuits, sunsets sink below candlelit tablescapes sprawling into star light. The last brimming serving dish is placed on the table between where he and I will be seated.

Chairs and people settle into the feast. Glasses raise. A toast to the guest of honour. I look across at him in opportunity to have his focus and ask how he is.

"Are you talking to me" he demeans.

It is a statement.

Not a question.

Incredulous chill spreads from his lips, a white cloud escapes crossing the dinner table. My mouth gapes from the blow. Our eyes meet for the first time in years, cadaverous hollows return my gaze and permeate through me. A hand lets go, gravy laden fork released from its hold. All fades in the forming mist, warmth leeching from everything surrounding us. Frost overtakes, seeping forward from him, crystalizing everything in its path. Its icy colourlessness coating the silverware and chalices in translucency. Parching the branching upon the wall, their succulent fruit shrivel and fall away. Like everything else.

The room darkens, all colour drained to bluing expanse of glacial breadth. Only him and I, and the barren mass encroaching the vastness from where he and I sit.

SNAP
The break of bones, ribs breaching
Bloodied thread holding the young flesh together let go
The threat that held everything in, unraveled
Everything fell apart
Which is real?
What's unfolding before you or the undoing inside you?
We're speaking miles now
Fake
The games we play with ourselves
The ugly parts of animals we hide
In front of us
Between us
Neither of us reached for the rope snaking away into our distance
His voice an alarm, bloodletting across ice
The carnivore feeding
Slavering rapt
Not the crushing feeling you'd expect
But illusory silence after the crash
Behind doors, coverings that shield open hearts hang in dark closets
A snap that catapults you to where you would not go
Everything held inside came to light
Permitting. Succumbing.
Old meat isn't tender
This beginning an end
In one moment, everything is different.
At 30 inches apart, everything that is not, is between us.

My eyes avert to the floor where the baby had thrown his peas minutes before. Pointing to it telling me it was a mess.

Yes.

The kitchen paint, curtains, art, rest upon the tiles laid on quicksand. The setting, all of it bandages masking ill preparation. A me I had not been for myself, a role played for agreements he excluded from our future. Creating self, outside oneself, my identity his mirror reflection. Like a flower needing watering, I had forgotten how to grow.

Breakfast, offspring, tight body, clean, errands, smile, pot roast.

Rewind. Repeat.

Rewind. Repeat.

Erase.

A stack of days behind us, another like the others. Except it isn't.

A fast car tearing away from navigated roads over a cliff into rough waters. Except it wasn't.

Flags raised on the beach; I entered the water anyway. What came to follow was being dragged, from self and everything around me. Pulled to sea, grasping for ground with fists of water. The more adamant I became, the last of what I had in my sight, moved farther away.

A beating swelling higher than the waves, blood pounding hard against my eardrums. Thoughts blurring in an oblivion of struggle. Swimming against a riptide is futile.

Exhausted, I had to give up and allow it to swallow me.

I let go.

Tranquility came, I've heard that about drowning, but I still felt air touching my face. Then I saw it, the current ahead and behind me. Do something else. I moved perpendicular away from the current, aligning self parallel to land, and eased into gentle lapping of the calm sea. When I regained my breath, I swam. When my feet could touch bottom, I stood.

Newly standing feet quickly learn to run.

A long day faded deep grey. We turn to one another, my hair blowing past my woolen shoulder onto the back of yours. A stone house far from home, in rubble behind us. Little lives we crafted. Save precociousness from oneself. Save him. Your eyes reflecting the evening's overcast back to me. All your problems were mine. Prisons, riddles, villains, heroes, a triumphant, and a loser. Memory is based on perception, and perception illudes sensibility and reveals the foolish. Unsubscribed to a sort of fairy tale, the ending a signature bottom line. I see me entirely different then who I saw myself in. The more I looked within, the clearer everything else was around me.

In one moment, my mind is made up.

Swimming with sharks requires thick skin, but young blood exposed raw heals in new layers. A paradox that what you need to learn, you learn from not knowing it. I let go of what I failed to grasp in hands squeezed tightly. Resolving to shift from force to ease. Fully submersed, giant waves dissipate to ebbs and flows.

These adventures sustain a soul long after they are lived. A traveller versus vacationer, soulmate versus friend, soaring instead of diving. Different viewpoints of things similar. Travel light taking with you what you need and leave the rest behind. Love grew in the exchange of moments converged and, in the grasses, covering the spanning distance between us.

This end, a beginning.

Start Today... Start Where You Are by Judith Loe

Radio blasting in the background "Hear it for New York!..New York, New York, New York..." With Alicia Keys' voice penetrating the bedroom, she stops midway packing her suitcase. A pang in her heart, tears welling in her eyes...Frozen in time her mind goes back to that first time their lips found each other.

In the arrival hall of JFK November 11. He emerged from the sliding doors that lead to the arrival hall. Tall, handsome with the Marlborough man look and an air of confidence and carelessness, he carried his duffle bag over his shoulder. She was struck by how the sight made her feel...Her nervousness and excitement elevated as she murmured to herself: "A....bsolutely gorgeous...." More striking than the man in the countless Skype calls that preceded this initial encounter.

She caught his eyes and he smiled as he approached her: "You are beautiful," his deep blue eyes looking straight into hers as he took her in and pulled her close. Melting in his arms, she had never felt anything like this...A combination of excitement, teenage flutters, and a feeling of wholeness .... it felt so good. She knew this is where she belonged.

The kiss, the song...the start of the most turbulent, romantic, passionate, dramatic life that was to follow. A dream come true; a nightmare come true...all wrapped into 9 years with the man she would call the love of her life. The love who would show her the meaning of "feeling alive" as she was faced with emotions, she never knew she could ever possess. It was a lesson in love, lust, and ecstasy...he allowed her to see what it meant to desire deeply, more than she ever thought possible. Making love with this man was like a scene in a movie, a scene women secretly swoon over. He made her feel sexy, beautiful, and desirable. Always wanting her and desiring her to be his, she surrendered...fully and completely. She had been waiting for this man all her life.

As the years with him had been marked by so many feelings of utter bliss, love and ...sorrow, they gave her the opportunity to grow, to live and to truly feel. Being with this man showed her what it means to feel all the emotions...the good ones, the bad ones... the deep passion and lust desire, deep love for a man, anger, anxiety, jealousy, fear, loneliness...

Loving him showed her how to be vulnerable and surrender to sensations she had never felt before nor did she think ever possible. She had meaningful relationships before, beautiful soul level relationships with men that gave her stability, friendship, and companionship. All of them were lovely. They were safe, they felt peaceful and calm. None of these relationships were this intense and none of them would take her to the depth of her soul.

It was as if she almost did not recognize herself and her soul started running the show more than ever. The love she felt for this man was one she had never experienced in her life. She loved intensely and she gave herself completely to him, just as he loved her and gave to her all that he was able to give her. Together, yet on opposite sides, they were coping with the same pains and the same insecurities. Both battling their demons within and in the process not able to digest what they saw in the other and ultimately within themselves. Both projecting onto one another, yet not understanding that in essence they were one in union pushing each other further and further apart.

The last years were marked by two people deeply in love, but growing apart. She found herself alone and lonely many times. Moments when he traveled, she felt alone... when he was home with her, she still felt alone. She felt she was taken for granted, not appreciated seen and often times not respected by the decisions he made that impacted them both. However, she was always there for him.

Why could he not be there for her when she needed him? He felt the pressure and acted out on her, often times met by her retaliated passive aggressiveness. The tension escalated and she grew increasingly somber and distant.

In her mind she believed she needed to be strong...not show or voice her displeasure. She was not taught to feel and express...she was not taught to be assertive and speak up, and therefore she retracted into a safe place, her own internal space, where she could hide in her silence. Silence to avoid confrontation, but suppress the honest expression of emotions.

Eventually all these suppressed emotions would rise to the surface involuntarily in ways that would not be pleasant... she did not know how to deal with them. Her stubbornness often fought against these inner confrontations. He showed her who she was and she did not like what she saw... She saw an insecure woman who felt the need to defend herself in order to be understood. Yet, she was not capable of expressing what she needed.

She often wondered, "How and why has it come to this?"

Eventually she realized something had to change. She loved this man so very much, but she felt unhappy inside. She wanted to feel joy with him again, the joy they both felt when times were so good, carefree, and loving. She knew she had to change...That's all she could do. She had to find out how she could take responsibility for her own actions, her own happiness and how she could decide to live her life.

If she could just take back the reins, and design her life the way she was intended to do, then surely their relationship would flourish once again. She had defined herself by the purpose of giving herself to him... She had done so from the beginning when he asked her to leave behind her career and her home to join him. And she followed him to the other side of the world. She had done so for love and wanted nothing but to be by his side...always.

But somewhere down the line she lost herself, she lost her central root. She believed that in order to feel loved and be safe she needed to send her roots and sense of value into him, and only him. She had redirected the central root that connected her to a healthy, grounded self and anchored it outside herself into something that could never give her the necessary grounded stability. She saw it, and she understood.

How wonderful would it be to create space and discover what each of them needed in order to heal themselves for the purpose of healing their relationship! With clarity and excitement, she waited for him to come home...everything would turn out perfect. She knew what she needed to do for herself and she knew that he needed to do the same for himself in order to grow back together. She was longing for the growth together for the sake of a relationship that could thrive in the connection. She was longing for the connection once again; longing to grow as two separate beings in order to come together as one. How blissful this would be...

She did not have to wait anymore.... the walk on the beach, the gloom on his face, his gaze on the footprints that left his marks in the sand, hands in his jeans pocket... not wrapped around hers...He stopped and once again, just like 9 years ago his deep blue eyes stared right into her. This time not with a look of admiration and love, but with stern intentions and deep sadness: "I can't do this anymore, I need to be on my own."

Once again, she melted...this time melted into disbelief and grief. Somehow, she knew this day would come, however always had held on to the belief that they were meant for each other and that their bond was indestructible. She thought that if she could change...he would too. She was wrong...

Her suitcase nearly packed, she stood up to find the letter he sent weeks after he left. Countless times she re-read his words, each time trying to find a clue about why he gave up on a life that could have been so amazing together.

My dearest,

I am sitting out on a bench on the river on a sunny morning looking at our Tower Bridge. Memories are flooding in. I have so many of them and all of them are so special. I write this letter to tell you that I love you and I hope my words will not be lost in translation. I do miss you; I have not forgotten you, nor will I ever. I am trying to move on but I'm finding it hard to compartmentalize my thoughts and memories of us. I know I have done you wrong by leaving you the way I did. In my mind there was no other option...but I am sorry for hurting you.

Darling, firstly don't think I blame you... it was just how it was. It was our situation and our dynamics. It was me...

To be very honest, I feel relief right now. I don't have to worry anymore. I am only looking after me now and don't have to worry about failing or upsetting you anymore. You were the best thing that ever happened to me, I mean it.

I think there is an expression about our life's journey (you know all these quotes better than I do). It says people and loved ones join your journey in life. Some get on to show you your way but sadly do not stay and they get off, but they were in your journey for a reason. There are tear drops running down my face as I write this. We did both try, I know there was never any hate or resentment between us, but rather our love and relationship had so many hurdles and misunderstandings and the real crack was the dynamics or yes, my dynamics....

Slowly she lowered the letter, her eyes stinging from the makeup that was now mixed with her tears.

Regardless of how much they loved each other...somehow, they did not love themselves enough to love the other completely and unconditionally. Both defined by their need to seek approval from the other, to be validated and fully accepted. She continued reading the letter:

"To be honest I think looking back, I felt I failed you very early on in our relationship. You had your way of dealing with things and I had mine. When it came to us, I just wanted to show you I was a success."

She was seeking his approval by nurturing him, caring for him and being anything he wanted her to be...She was seeking validity, respect, and attention from him...While he was working endless hours, traveling, and trying to make his mark in business. For him success would be the one thing that gave him validity and status. He identified himself by his success, wealth, and status... With the absurd perception that he had failed her, he was not able to stay with her as she was a constant reminder of his failures...It all made sense.

Two perfectly imperfect people who loved each other...Somehow, they could not be together. They knew each needed to head onto their own path of healing and self-discovery. Learning how to love and understand themselves first. How she would have loved to take the journey to wholeness together...in unity and love.

"No," she shook her head, "This was not meant to be."

It would have never worked out together. With all the wonderful journeys they have taken together, this journey will need to be taken alone. She gently touched the inscribed bracelet he gave her on her birthday. He had it engraved especially for them "Embrace the Unknown" it read, together with their initials...H&P.

He would always be in her heart. In the past, they had hurt each other tremendously and the pain will never be forgotten...but she choose to go forth in radiance and will release the old stories of sorrow and wrong doing in order to grow and illuminate light as a Warrior goddess, an Empress of love.

She was ready to rewrite her story! She was ready to release him...with fondness still in her heart... always.

Into the world energy, she said, "I thank you for the 9 meaningful unforgettable years you have given me my love. It is time to say goodbye".

Now...

With the wisdom gained she is ready to explore and find out if the free spirit that is deep within is ready to manifest. Is she able to face her fears and go into unknown territory to live life the way she is intended to live? She feels the cheer and laughter from her 8 sisters enveloping her like a warm blanket of pure love and encouragement. Each lovely face popping up in front of her, smiling at her and nodding with approval as she gathers the courage to detach from the memories of her past in order to create the vision of her limitless future.

Fondly, she recollects the time they met, her 8 soul sisters. On a virtual soul connection encounter that was surely destined and orchestrated by universal energy. Each so unique, from various cultures and different parts of the world...she recognizes a sliver of her own self in each. They never have met physically, never been able to give each other a hug...However, the energy of the power of 9 has broken the physical barrier with love, compassion, and collective unity. With such feelings of gratefulness, she acknowledges that the gift she has received during her most challenging time, is the unity and power of the

9 sisters...A bond that is experienced only in the essence of 9 radiant women creating incredible alchemy and empowerment.

Tomorrow is the day...The big leap into the unknown future. Excited, with a hint of fear unease and worry she goes through her checklist: house key in the lock box, the house is spotless and ready to be shown to prospective buyers. It won't take much time before the house will be sold. The beautiful views of The Pacific Ocean flanked by palm trees are the highlight of this home. She remembers sitting on the deck witnessing many magical sunsets. The newly renovated kitchen with all the latest gadgets...a food lover's dream...

She remembers, just two years ago, her heart was skipping a beat when he gifted her the Pacific Ocean dream kitchen. The one thing she always dreamed of, a kitchen where she would create and invent new recipes to share with dear friends and family. One lucky chef will be cooking fabulous meals here...One lucky couple will make this their nest. Perhaps it was not meant to be for them in this lifetime, perhaps not this time around.

She takes one last look at the empty house, once filled with laughter and happy moments. Now merely a shell of past memories... Her heart is heavy, but her spirits are high. For her this chapter has come to an end. It's time for a new cycle...she is ready to embrace it.

Where she is heading, she doesn't know...All she has is her suitcase and a one-way ticket to her new destination of LIMITLESS potentials. There is nothing that is holding her back, nothing that tethers her to a place, a person, or obligations... The world is her oyster and tomorrow she will jump right in.

"Sisters, here I come! Are you ready for a brand-new start? Our journey to wholeness is about to commence!"

A Soul's Journey By Heidi C. Tyler

Flick the switch will you sweetie?

'Which switch are you talking about,'   Nixie asked.

The one on the wall.

'Yes, but which wall do you mean,' Nixie pleaded.

The one that connects us all to the universe of course!

'I didn't know there was such a thing,' Nixie replied.

Oh, I thought everyone knew how to connect to the universe. I learnt it many lives ago.

'Lives! We only get one life, don't we?' Nixie cried.

Ah well, let me tell you a story.

'Ooh I love stories,' Nixie whispered.

Long ago I was a male warrior, looked up to by the tribe and completely loyal to the king. My warriors and I fought many battles protecting everyone in the kingdom. We weren't treated well by the Royal Family and my warriors weren't happy. One day one of my warriors, a very brave man, was beaten by the king. He didn't fight back and took such a severe beating that it blinded him.

'OMG, but why?' Nixie shouted.

Simply because he hadn't done the king's bidding fast enough!

It was the final straw for me, and I killed the king. I ordered his family to leave and never return. I had the full support of the tribe and I went on to rule them with compassion and care. I also got to enjoy the material things of life and became dependent on others, as well as becoming very unfit. My people were overrun by another band of warriors and I was killed in the attack.

Nixie screamed, 'Oh no, killing the king was such a dreadful thing to do. Though I kind of understand why you did it. They hadn't shown kindness toward their people. It sounds like you really cared about the people and did your best for them, but what I don't understand is why you became unfit and allowed another band of warriors to take over?'

Yes, I did care, and I'd been so strong defending the tribe, but it became so easy to forget what was truly important. Perhaps losing my own life was the price I had to pay!

'What happened after you died?' Nixie asked.

I moved on to my next incarnation.

'So, who were you next? I hope it wasn't a murderer,' Nixie remarked.

My next life was as a woman living in the Middle East. The place was Samaria and it was 1st century BC. I was a Samaritan born to a lowly family where I was forced to work in a different community. I was disliked and treated badly for the whole of my life. I held onto my faith and stayed above the anger I felt despite all the struggles of having such a hard life. I gave my all to everything I did, but because I was considered different, I suffered all the time at the hands of people who thought they were better than me. I knew life was to be lived and felt sure the reward would come. When I reached the age of 25, I wasn't married and had no protection.

'Why did you need protection? What happened to you?' Nixie asked fearfully.

I was grabbed by a group of men before I got back to my room, and they raped me. It was so violent, and they left me for dead. No-one came to help me, and I died.

'Oh no,' Nixie cried. 'No woman should ever have to suffer like that. Please tell me your next life was something beautiful and loving.'

Well, my next life took me to China, where I was a lowly servant, badly treated and with very little to eat. The only way I could get any food was to run errands for others in the village, seeking food as payment. It was an incredibly hard life getting from one day to the next and I died young but had learnt so much from the connections I'd made.

'What a dreadful life. I dare not ask about the next one,' Nixie sobbed.

In my next life, my soul connected me with a very wealthy family. I wanted for nothing and met people who taught me about buying and selling. I built up expertise to make money of my own. I connected with people all over the world. So many cultures, faiths, and ways of living. I lived well and never wanted for anything. Except that's not true. I did want more. I wanted to feel the connection to something that had eluded me. A connection to another. I had no view of what that might feel like. Sadly, I passed never knowing in that lifetime what that could have been.

As my soul never ends, I moved into my next life. A life of service and duty. I'd brought my life learning from my past lives and gave it my all. I became highly regarded and enriched with accolades. I cared for everyone I met. I connected with so many but once again didn't make the connection I sought. Again, my life came to an end.

'I just don't know what to say. I hope this next one is better,' Nixie gasped.

In my next life, my soul wanted to find more beauty. The beauty it gave me was connecting through poetry. The poetry of love that unites our souls across the globe. With its strength and power, its connection can alter the world through pure energy of words.

'Oh, I love poetry!' exclaimed Nixie. 'Where were you?'

I was in 9th Century Persia.

'Persia, I've never heard of such a place.' Nixie's brow furrowed in confusion.

Oh, it's got a different place name now. It's called Iran.

'I think I prefer the name Persia. It's far more poetic,' Nixie declared.

Oh, I agree. I poured out my heart in my writing and unbeknown to me it captured hearts all over the world. It became my greatest gift connecting so many with love in their hearts. And yet, the love I searched for was still unfound.

'Where can I read your poems?' Nixie asked.

Oh, I expect they're on the internet somewhere. Just look up Sufism poetry. You'll find many beautiful poems and who knows, some of them might be mine!

'What happened next?' Nixie asked.

As my soul entered my next life, I arrived in 15th century Europe.

'Were you a man or woman?' Nixie asked.

A woman.

'A rich, famous and talented woman I hope,' Nixie screeched.

Sadly, not rich or famous. I was from a poor family and because I was the youngest, I was sent to work.

'So, you were talented!' Nixie exclaimed.

Well yes, but not in the way you might think. I was able to tell people when things were going to happen.

'What... like premonitions?' Nixie asked.

Not exactly. I was able to make predictions and they always turned out to be right. I worked in a very rich house and the owner kept taking me round and getting paid money for my predictions. My fame spread around quickly into neighbouring towns. I even got visited by the Lord.

'Rubbing shoulders with the high and mighty now I see,' laughed Nixie

Yes, but the Lord didn't like what I was able to do. He was a deeply religious man and took me to the castle. The priest thought I interacted with the devil. I didn't know anything about any devil and just knew I was connected in ways they couldn't understand.

'What did you do?' Nixie asked.

I tried to tell the priest, but I wasn't as clever as he was. Priests were educated and I wasn't, but I knew my soul was connected to everything. I wasn't connected as a Christian soul, but as an energy. An energy they just couldn't see or understand.

'Did they kill you?' Nixie asked tentatively.

Well, I know I died, but I don't actually recall how that happened.

'Maybe it was a peaceful one. Let's hope so. Where to next?' Nixie squealed.

My next life was as a woman, in a perfectly normal family in the early 18th century. In Southern Italy no less.

'Oh, thank goodness for that. It's about time you were normal.' Nixie laughed.

It was certainly a lot more pleasant than many of my earlier lives. This time I lived in a port town and I got interested in trade. As I grew up, I found work with some merchants and discovered I had a talent and it fit with how I saw the world operating.

'How was that?' Nixie asked.

Well by having trade that allows everyone to benefit, and that is carried out fairly! Everyone looking out for each other, without fear and conflict.

'We need some of that now. Can you start this concept again in this life, please,' Nixie pleaded.

Well, I did go on to become very successful and wealthy when I was quite young. I was ahead of my time; however, it came at a price.

'Oh no, you're not killed again are you,' Nixie cried.

No, I wasn't. I enjoyed my life, but I never experienced the love of another.

'I've just realised, you've not married or had children in any of these past lives. That is so sad,' Nixie said.

I could see Nixie was about to say something, so I quickly interjected.

My next life put me into a seafaring family, in pre-Victorian era, just before the Battle of Waterloo. I was sent to school and then to the Academy of the Royal Navy.

Nixie's eyes lit up in recognition. 'Hang on a minute, you live in a Royal Navy town now. How uncanny.'

Yes, I do!

I learnt it's important to protect everyone although some

people are not able to behave responsibly toward others. I served the state for quite some time, but not all of the actions we were asked to perform made me feel comfortable. I did progress and became captain of my own ship.

'Oh wow, I wish I could see your ship now,' stated Nixie.

I travelled to the Indian Ocean to quell a riot. When we got there, we found villagers and nothing more. My instructions were to burn their crops and destroy their village.

'I sincerely hope you didn't do that!' Nixie screamed.

No, I didn't. I found out that the Empire had wanted it done because they decided to take the province from the Indian prince. They had become corrupt and greedy. I learned a valuable lesson. For many, it is almost impossible for power not to corrupt.

'What did you do?' Nixie asked.

I made sure the people were moved from their village before it got flattened. No deaths occurred while this hateful deed was carried out. I died with a huge regret on my soul and vowed I would never work for a corrupt state again.

'Where to next'? Nixie questioned.

This life, I smiled.

'Really?' Nixie said, looking almost disappointed.

But why so glum?

'Well, I know most of this life,' Nixie told me.

OK, tell me what you think you know.

'You were born in England. You had a hard time at school. The teacher and headmistress beat you because you were different. You had varying illnesses and problems with your health. You found love. They found someone else to love, so you lost your love. You found love again but that ended too. I guess that's not surprising as you hadn't learnt anything about actual real love in your previous lives. You found love a third time and had a child, which was an absolute joy for you.

You had a highly successful career, no doubt because of everything you'd learnt in your past lives! You enjoyed the finer things in life but made yourself ill. So much so, you had to stop doing the very job you loved. You had no-one else to blame but yourself really.

You moped about for two years, being utterly pathetic, until you found your way and started to sort your life out.

You banged on about wanting to better yourself and went on a personal development journey. You even showed off some new skills you'd learnt. Juggling and reciting a huge chunk of the periodic table, which you'd never known before. You even taught some young kids in a school how to do juggling.

Then you did a load of energy medicine stuff. That made a huge change for you and your body completely transformed. All your ill health was completely eradicated.

Finally, you created your 12 category Lifebook. You worked through all your past negative beliefs, took control of your emotions, and even wrote a book all about it. You went from being a grumpy person with no outlook on life to being an inspiring, vibrant, and happy person with friends all over the world. You've inspired others by showing them you can turn anything around if you really want to.'

Have you finished?

'Yep, I think that sums it up,' Nixie said proudly.

Well, there is a significant chunk at the end I need to tell you about.

I didn't consciously remember all that I'd learnt from my

past and yet there were connections within me that came to the fore in this life when I raised my consciousness. I repeated some fundamental mistakes, but learnt we have to look deeply at the negative moments, to find what they are trying to teach us and then find the positives within them. More importantly we need to become conscious of what we are doing and why.

I value recognition for people who do things for the greater good. I used this during my entire career, wanting my team to be recognised for their hard work and the value they gave.

I learnt how to build my own protection, which carried through into early childhood in this life. I taught myself to thrive despite the hard times.

I learnt all about trade and creating wealth. I created wealth for others throughout my entire career and sufficient enough wealth for myself and family. Yes, I spent years of my life living emotions to the full, but finally found how to manage them well.

It's interesting that I had written poetry. I loved writing poetry as a child but let it slip from my grasp. I'm picking up where I left off through the beauty of reading poetry. Who knows, I may end up reading my own writing from back then. I'd explained feelings and emotions during that time, and now within my own published book, I've written everything about them through my own writing. That feels so right.

My gift of being able to make predictions continued into this life. I predicted my own near fatal car accident. It frightened me so much that I suppressed it. Now I appreciate my own intuition and use it as often as I can. Instead of suppressing my intuition, I'm encouraging and nurturing it.

I was condemned as being different and now I'm comfortable with it for the first time in my entire life.

I'm truly connected to my soul. Not as a religious soul, but through the power of my own energy. An energy that is connected to the entire universe and beyond.

I appreciate everyone's gifts and contribution, even if it's at odds with my own. You see everyone is right, and no-one is wrong. We are all just different and need to learn to engage with each other. Not just physically, but energetically. We need to learn about our differences and how to interact better.

I was captain of my own ship and now I am captain of my own life. I learnt that being instructed to harm others didn't fit with the values and beliefs I hold dear. That hasn't changed. My values and beliefs are at the very core of my being.

Nixie thought about this for a second. 'What messages would you give to others?'

Love yourself first, then you can help others. Showing loyalty to others must fit with your own core values and beliefs and not be at your own expense.

Show love, kindness, care and compassion to everyone, no matter who they are. Reflect your mirror on to them, so they may learn from you.

Everything comes your way so you can learn and become a better person. Be conscious of what you are doing and why. Accept others for who they are too. We are each on our own journey and living in our own reality. Nothing is good, or bad!

Educate yourself with whatever excites you and fills your heart with joy, and have fun doing it too. Create your own expertise and use it to create value for yourself and to serve the greater good. Appreciate and recognise the value you, and the people around you, create. There is wealth around the world, and there is nothing wrong with creating value for others and gaining wealth for yourself. Just don't let wealth turn into greed and power!

Don't be afraid to create boundaries in your life. Be clear on your beliefs and values. How you live your life is entirely your choice. Don't let others take that away from you or dictate how you should be or live. Speak and live by your own truth.

Learn about your emotional life. Learn and understand the triggers for your thoughts and learn how to free yourself from negativity. Your thoughts create your emotions. Show gratitude for all the positive things in life. These are what bring positive emotions.

Connect with your soul by listening to and trusting your intuition. You have an energetic connection that is far more powerful than you can possibly imagine. The more aware you become the more you can manifest the future life you are seeking. Your soul is connected to a benevolent universe.

Celebrate being different. Be proud of being who you are. Tap into your own source of energy and let your light shine.

Look after your health and well-being through self-care. Create your natural state of inner calm enjoying joy, peace, quiet and freedom every time you need it. Nourish your mind, body, and spirit.

We love being part of a tribe. Create or become part of a community of like-minded people who you can interact and engage with. One that is supportive and there when you need them. I am part of the greatest community there could ever be.

I am part of 'The Sisterhood'.

'Who are The Sisterhood?' Nixie gasped.

A group of 9 women who came together all so incredibly different. It ought not to work, but it does on every level, because we all learnt what it means to show love, kindness, gratitude, support, acceptance, collaboration, integrity and how to interact and engage with each other. We help each other through tough times, without judgement or ego. In fact, a group who have every positive value you would ever want in your ultimate best friend. A group of 9 who joined together on their path to wholeness.

Nixie, each life goes by so quickly, so we need to use our time wisely and with the right people.

'What if someone is afraid to take the next step?' Nixie asked.

Just take baby steps every day toward the life you dream of. Every step will take you that bit closer. Before you know it you'll have stepped forward a lot. You won't believe how far you've come.

'I don't have much time left, so what do you want me to do now?' Nixie asked

I want you to say, 'It's Time To ....'

'It's Time To .... What?' Nixie sighed

It's Time to .... Celebrate.

'What are we celebrating?' Nixie enquired.

A future that is so incredible and powerful, that it is filled with love, joy, harmony, and amazing individuals who, when they are together, can heal themselves and each other. Can lift each other up to incredible heights. Can push each other forward to achieve things they never thought were possible.

A group that keeps on growing and giving. Who inspire others and themselves. Who stand in a room and exude a sense of purpose and fulfilment. Who fill the room with light and energy, creating a wave of positive emotion that is absorbed by everyone.

That's what we're celebrating. It will be the greatest celebration event the world has ever seen.

'WOW, can I come?' Nixie pleaded.

Journey to Wholeness by Yvette Simpson

When I was at the bottom of the deep blue sea, I had no notion if I was alive or dead, if I was breathing in water or not needing to breathe at all. Where was the surface anyhow? Was there even a boat to climb into or was there Land? It was such a desperate, soul crushing feeling that I could not easily describe it to anyone without feeling like a complete and total failure of a human being.

The journey back to wholeness began at the bottom of the ocean. I had not met Kali Ma then; I did not even know she existed deep within me, with the ferocity of a lioness, the stealth of a tigress and the patience of an elephant. I did not know ME.

I would love to tell you this is a story of flowers and rainbows and fairy tales, that my journey to wholeness, to get to meeting my own true Soul was one of sunshine and happiness but that would be flat out lying. I could embellish the truth and tell you there were some challenging days that were difficult but what would be the point? How would you, the Reader, feel the authenticity of my words or the completion of my journey?

I want to tell you all instead about Kali Ma, how she has helped me to become ME, the true me. She is the version of me who shows up in her own indomitable style and spirit. The journey to wholeness came about through the intensity of the pain and the sheer longevity of the horribleness of the situation I found myself in.

Let us skip the first 42 years of my life shall we and get to the crux of where I want to begin with this journey. This is a very brief overview but suffice to say, my marriage had broken down, 19 years of a relationship finished. This was the great love of my life and to boot I had two children pretty much oblivious to the ensuing maelstrom that would become their lives, two precious dogs left behind with my ex-husband, two businesses closed, moving halfway round the world only to journey back home to a house that was never supposed to be my home.

It was not supposed to be this way, I had done everything right or so I believed. I was so consumed by this love that I loved with all my heart, I loved unconditionally. I gave everything I had; physically, mentally, intellectually, emotionally, and spiritually. When it finally shattered, I literally was left with nothing, feeling so broken and beyond repair that it almost felt like there were just so many pieces spread out so far away that I would never, ever find myself again or worse I could not recover mentally.

My daily mantra began with - How the HELL did I get here? THIS is NOT my beautiful life. I have not completed degrees and master's in education, killed myself working all the hours God sent for those bits of paper and building up businesses, a portfolio of investments and sacrificing so much

TIME with my family to have lost SO MUCH. Thus ensued a mental and emotional breakdown (or breakthrough!) of gargantuan proportions.

I could not make any decisions either small or large - ranging from decisions about what to cook, how to take a train or even to just keep a straight thought in my head. I thought the panic attacks were a sign I had a brain tumour, but I was afraid to get a diagnosis and then face that reality instead. I did not even know at that point that it was a panic attack. I genuinely believed that we would all be better off at the end of the Deep Blue Sea and that there was nothing left but to save us all and die. I was incredibly lucky; I went to see my amazing family doctor who realised this was potentially a critical situation and she intervened immediately. I got medication and counselling treatment.

My two precious and unbelievable children were bewildered, and the ripple effects were catastrophic. Three years of family therapy ensued; it would take a completely different story to tell you about that journey all in of itself so let us stick to this one instead. When I finally started to come out of the fog of depression after the initial six months of treatment, I set one intention. This was totally different than anything I had ever wanted before.

I wanted to be truly, deeply contented within my own Soul – I did not believe it was a big ask but in the intervening years I have discovered that it is SOME journey. I realized that the superficial lifestyle - "having it all," that had looked so great on paper was nothing.

It had been built on sand with no deep foundation. I realised that I had always been searching, there had always been something just a little beyond my reach, I was always not quite "happy." No matter what new degree I gained, what bigger home, what amazing vacation or new business venture I took on, there was always something missing in ME.

Enter Kali Ma.

During a morning meditation, whilst really asking God (or the Universe or my Guardian Angels or anyone at all of a Higher Consciousness who might be listening) "how can I truly find inner peace?", my phone rang. In that moment, I was very put out but it was my Mum, but also obviously, I took the call. While we were chatting away it occurred to me how truly incredible my mum is. It was amazingly simple, I always knew it and was in awe of her but there was something different that day, it just sat differently inside of me.

My mum interrupting me on the meditation just as I was asking my question led me to do a search on powerful women. Starting to Google information about powerful women, and lo and behold, I found an article about Kali Ma – the divine mother, the Dark Mother, the Terrible Mother. She is a Hindu goddess of time, creation, preservation, and destruction. She rides a lion, her fair flows freely, she wears a garland of severed heads and a skirt of dismembered arms. She is also the most compassionate of all the goddesses. - BOOM! I took it as my sign from the Universe.

To find inner peace I needed a strong woman inside of me. I needed to take on the identity of Kali Ma and to fight all the demons inside me, surrounding me and waiting to devour me.

What happened next? I decided to channel my own Kali Ma. I called on her daily to help me take on a new identity and to fight back. I fought the banks for my home, at times that felt like an unwinnable stupid daily struggle. It took a huge amount of energy, and it almost broke me. I fought in court for my divorce and everything that entailed. It took four years; it was not pretty or pleasant. It made me stronger, but I was always "fighting", ready for the next war and on guard to step up to take on a battle.

I kept on searching through me to find that inner peace, that total Zen of tranquil bliss inside my own Soul - trying to meditate, trying to become a yogi - you name it. I had already become a Reiki Master, an IET Master, an NLP practitioner and yet there was something missing. In 2018, I lost my amazing, incredible mum to brain cancer and the world literally tilted and something inside me shifted imperceptibly.

I lost a year to grief; it was a constant immoveable unwanted companion, and I knew I had to come to terms with it. So, whilst searching yet again, I discovered yet another self-help course, that spoke of giving you the tools to transform your life. I loved the ethos of what it showed about living a smart life. I truly felt connected to the woman who spoke; her words and her energy and how she was completely at one in her own femininity, yet unbelievably strong and centered in her own soul. I felt like she was a living Kali Ma. This was another sign from the Universe.

I signed up. I played fully into the course for the six weeks and I began to look at every single aspect of my life in a totally different manner. I gifted myself the time required to really do the deep introspective work required. I discovered the three keys to success were self- discipline, consistency, and persistence. If you want to lose weight, if you want to save money, if you want to change an aspect of your character, lose a bad habit – anything you want to achieve within realistic terms can be achieved with those three keys.

This course had many different areas of your life to focus on and I really took this to heart. I have loved writing since I was a kid. I could combine one of my favourite hobbies whilst creating a life vision and wrapping that around a smarter life structure. It came at a good time in my life.

Fast forward six months of deep introspection into my Life and I suddenly realised that I had been playing at half speed all my life. I had also noticed over the past number of years through observing people that I met through various self-help courses that we had one thing in common. We were searching outside instead of inside. I came to a terrifying conclusion. I realised I needed Self-Love, to find Inner Peace and Soul Healing, I needed to really love my own self, inside and out.

All my fighting, all my Kali Ma strength and ferocity was needed to go on a journey to heal my own Self. For as long as I can remember I have been fighting, life has been one long battle after another. Nothing came easy and through deep introspection and examination of my own character, values, beliefs, and rules I realised that I needed to *surrender*. I needed to change my identity in some ways, let go of old self-limiting beliefs, create a new, empowered mindset that questioned every negative thought that passed through my brain.

This became my Mantra.

2020 became the year of Self Love and Surrender. I began to look at the smallest of things with the greatest of respect and gratitude. For example, I thanked the Universe for the sky and how incredibly beautiful it is, a rainbow, a sunset, a moon beam. I thanked the Universe for the big things such as I was grateful that my brain and every other single part of my physical self was in perfect working condition, instead of focusing on trivial things such as, "oh I look old, I'm getting wrinkles."

I changed every sentence to thank the Universe that I am still here to raise my kids; thank it too that everyone I love is healthy. That really shifted my focus and my identity. I had less time for the haters, the people who wanted to bitch and moan about things in life that were meaningless, like a coffee being delivered with the wrong cup or the line of traffic ahead on the commute. I felt more connected to the Universe in a way I had never felt before - to believe that my thoughts became my own reality and it was important to keep a positive connection to the entire Universe.

I moved away from toxic friendships and relationships that made me feel small or inadequate. I "gave" myself the gift of freedom to enjoy my own company, to schedule "alone" time to write, to meditate, to just be in the now. I found 8 Soul Sisters through the journey, who are their own unique Kali Ma's and who have empowered me to step into my own centre of authenticity; they allowed me the sacred space to grow in a supportive and protected arena. The power of Nine has been overwhelming.

I found joy in the relationships I already held dear in my life. I invested quality time and energy into them in an authentic and honest way. Now, every single time one of my kids ask me a question, I genuinely stop and put down my phone and really listen. I had spent my life being "busy," I think my byline was "Give me 5 minutes" because I was always in the middle of doing something.

I found that time with people I really love has changed.

Quality time became even more deep and meaningful just by really looking at them when they spoke. I listened to every single word they said and not wanting to "fix" their lives or jump in with solutions to their problems. I found that by simply holding space for them to speak and to hear them authentically has made the relationships so much more connected and deeper.

I realised too that Kali Ma is willing and she is capable of doing the necessary things that others fear. She can destroy egos and happily kill demons, but her love is SO fierce that she destroys evil so that she can grant freedom. I LIVE FREE. I have independence, I have love in every area of my life and even more importantly, I have balance. I truly live on my own terms and it feels amazing.

Kali Ma reminds me to live in the NOW, to enjoy how temporary this body and this life is. She reminds me to enjoy the beauty of life and everything in it because death is a certainty and we do not know how much time we have left. Knowing so deeply with every fibre in my being that this Life is such a precious gift has awakened in me an endless well of gratitude.

I AM deeply contented within my own Soul; I am still on a journey, but this one is vastly different. I have found peace within. I will always work on my personal life vision, but I have realised that it is merely a map. I am the one who steers the journey and when life throws curve balls how I respond is more important. I have my one true north star to guide me and support me. I can see the transformations that have happened across all areas of my Life from the relationships I now nurture and cherish to my health and fitness, my financial life, my spirituality and beyond. My future is comprised of the following, my own mindset that I guard ferociously, the daily choices I make and the actions that I take every day in every area of my life. I still have challenges and I still have moments where I slip back a little in my thought process, but I know now that my own mindset can pivot instantaneously and that is my choice. I have the ability and a toolkit of emotional and mental hacks to switch my mindset and shift my state in seconds.

What really makes me immensely and deeply contented is that I know at a deep cellular level that the people in my life now love and support me unconditionally and want only the best for me. The Universe has my back, it wants me to succeed but even though I believe that when I put things in context, I am but a grain of sand in a vast galaxy of planets – I matter and my Life has meaning.

LIFE IS SWEET!

The Journey Back Home by Smadar Asraf

And it calls us towards it, the wondrous creation. It is an inherent, innate calling that has existed in us since time immemorial. Calling of a 'place' we never really left and never left us.

We are drawn to it, longing to experience the totality of existence. Be one with the universe. The journey is conscious. The desire - to merge. Experience love, be love, live.

We were ejected into the world at birth. Our arrival here devoured the cards. We have found ourselves in different and varied realities of life. Even if they are supportive, many times inadvertently and sometimes brutally, expropriated our uniqueness from us when we had to respond to the dictates of the various frameworks in which we grew up and in which we live today.

To use a simplistic metaphor, think of water and oil where each has its own nature. If we devour them together, we get a seemingly mixed liquid. Our life, for all the mixes and effects that are applied to us with the true nature of each of them preserved and returned to its natural source as soon as they are allowed to be without interference. Thus, the unique soul of ours scrambled into our own life experience - if we let it be –

remembers its true nature. Thus, it is refined and collected to itself while expressing its wondrous uniqueness in the world.

We live out of longing

We live out of deep longing. The supreme desire seeks to illuminate our paths and constantly signals us of its 'place', invites us to it and illuminates our journey on the way back home, to ourselves, to it, to the stillness and wholeness of the all-embracing all that contains us within it. Which always contained us.

Responsiveness to longing can be defined in earthly concepts of love, self-love, self-fulfillment, self-discovery, personal development, and growth. All of these are verses and definitions that express in human words the way back home - to ourselves, in which we feel lighter and more uplifted.

In order to move towards this Heavenly experience out of the tumultuous reality in which most of us find ourselves, we need to develop attention and focus. We want to learn how we interfere with the wonderful being that we are, to manifest in the world and stop it in order to allow it to flourish and prosper.

In addition, we want to pay attention to all the 'isness' that surrounds us:

Next to every sadness lies joy, next to every scarcity there is abundance, next to every confusion there is clarity and next to every pain lies relief. It is our attention and our choice of what to pay attention to that shapes our life experience. We are required to understand what we want and where we are heading to but things are not always clear in advance. When you have a general direction, move, and everything else will be revealed to you later. Trust it.

The road is revealed while in motion

It's possible to liken it to moving towards a certain town you do not know. It has one house you want to get to, but you do not quite know where it is located. In any case, you start moving towards the town and when you reach it, it is already much easier to locate the specifics you are looking for. The same is true when it comes to realization and self-fulfillment: you do not always need to know all the details of your plan in advance in order to execute it, things will get clearer on the go. As we make moves toward our destination, we will understand what are the specific wishes throughout the path we seek to accomplish.

We assume there is someone who knows the answers

For the most part, our attention is scattered. We do not know what we want and where we are going. Many times, we do not even know why we are here and what we do here on the ball? Who runs the affairs? Who are you asking? What is the direction? What should guide our behavior? And more. We assume that there is someone who knows the answers and we pray to encounter them in order to free ourselves from all question marks. This is why we turn to religion or the exact sciences, we look for answers. Both religion and physics try to understand the universe, the source of matter, where we came from, what we have compromised and provide an answer to these existential questions. Physics tries to do this even without involving matters of faith, destiny, luck and so on.

Feeling good is a lofty goal, it is not a luxury

'Gentle but stubborn whispers' sought to direct my way. Is it a desire? will? guidance? intuition?

I learned to respond in a positive manner to what makes me feel good, personally, specifically. I realized that I have an influence on how I feel, and that it is a function of what I choose - even if unconsciously - to pay attention to. I realized that sometimes my attention is present and sometimes it's absent within my life, depending on what I am dealing with and how secure or unsecure I feel.

I learned that feeling good is a lofty goal. It is not a shame to strive towards it and it is not a luxury. I learned that it's right for me to check what I want to absorb into myself and what not to, what I take from life and what I give up, and that it's right to reject what I do not want even if it's a lot of things. I found out that out of all 'what I am not,' reveals to me what I am.

Intuition is a powerful guide

I learned to be attentive to intuition, to the acceptance and decipherment of intra-personal messages without voluntary thinking, and responsiveness to that inner pulse. Intuition is a powerful guideline in our cognitive journey back home. It can stand Stubborn against any rationalization.

Stubborn intuition guided me years ago to stay away from a 20-year-old soulmate, who loved me very much and was dear to my heart, but the desire to stay away and avoid meeting her pressed me. We had some unresolved issues between us that could not be addressed and I could no longer force myself to act contrary to my gut feeling. I could not explain exactly what was deterring me so much, but I knew I wanted to stay away until we disconnected. It felt right then - 10 years ago and it feels right today after going through inner work and digestion. I guess I will always have a warm place in my heart for her.

We better learn to avoid energetic black holes that suck our energy on our journey back home, otherwise we will be swallowed up in them, light years away from our destination which is living to the fullest. Relationships that drag you down must come to an end.

Our release from the shackles of the past is possible and at our reach

Our attention and the choice of how to use it **do not depend on external factors.** Our liberation from the shackles of the past, from historical conclusions and limiting beliefs, is possible and within our power. Every movement, every growth, stems from paying attention to some wrong action that we do and stopping it. Attention and focus are tools to calibrate, distill, and train on a daily basis.

Our journey is a journey of recollection

Prayer connects us with the totality of existence, with the great power, the source of all things, and with ourselves. Prayer enables unmediated direct speech with the embracing-all intelligence in which we take part. **Our journey across life is a journey of remembering our true essence.** The essence I call home - supreme intelligence. Everything that is necessary for the journey is already within us and at our reach.

Home - the real one - is pulsating within us

Home is not just a place; home is an experience. Home is warmth, security, and protection. Sometimes the memory of home is weak and distant because our life experiences were or are, very difficult and challenging, but even then, from a distance, home – the innate one - beats within us, lives and exists, sends pulses of vitality, signals us where to turn, which way to take, who to talk to and what to do. Developing listening to the guidance and intuition that comes from within our being is critical to the journey. It allows us to respond to the call and develop a system of trust in ourselves and in life.

Pain is an ally

Pain is an integral part of our existence. **Pain is an ally** that is taking good care of us. Pain is not personal, it marks a boundary, it marks in the body and mind the effect of false and limiting beliefs that we live according to. Sometimes it's an expression of a live and real wound. In any case, it is there to inspire us to make a move towards ourselves. Always.

If for example, I grew up in a violent atmosphere and repeatedly reacted to it with a gathering of the body into a cocoon, there's a chance I will move on to adulthood with a head hunched over, sometimes suffering from migraines and shoulder pain that petrified due to years of training in closures. This actual pain tells me that I'm doing something wrong with my body posture and asks me to find the way to stand up straight again from within.

Life vision pulls us to it

In the face of the peace relationship we develop with pain,

we better have a life vision even if it is general, even if it is only experiential. After years of being single, it was the pain of being alone that pushed me to a journey of searching love within and out (which is always one). It was only the knowing of how I wanted to feel in my next relationship, that I held in my attention. I gave up every item on my 'grocery list' regarding who my spouse should be and focused on the feeling I was inviting into my life when the person showed up. I focused on how our 'together' would feel.

If I had held all those beliefs of who this man was supposed to be, we would not be together today. I believe I was drawn into such a beautiful love life at age 46 because I focused on the vision I had for a relationship - it was clear to me how I wanted to feel in the relationship. Otherwise, I could not explain how I connected with a person light years away from me in so many things, but a total partner to the paradise we've created.

Even our most limiting beliefs can be changed

The power of limiting beliefs is strong and powerful. Sometimes we manage to convince ourselves that this is the way things really are, that if I live in an experience of scarcity out of a belief that "I will never have enough money," it will probably be the case in the future as well. That even though I really want a partner, if I believe that "I do not deserve it," it will not happen. But even our most limiting beliefs can be dissolved, disassembled, and we can develop new ones instead, which brings good emotional experiences. For that kind of work, we will use inquiry and attention. When you are in times of hardships, check out where in your wonderful and smart body you are holding yourself, where does it hurt? Where is the distress?

Even the smallest finding of pain location will serve you as a tip of the thread back inward into the experience of totality.

Your body is trying to tell you something

Focusing and paying attention to pain and agreeing to experience and allow it, to illuminate it for a moment instead of running away from it or trying to get rid of it, creates a change in it. It is right to let pain be and try to acknowledge why it is here and what is it actually asking for? You want to feel different, you're groundbreaking. But before heading out into a district of new experience, it is right to let what is currently there be, even if it hurts.

We better remember that **even our most stubborn beliefs have been learned somewhere in our lives and as we have learned to produce them, we can also learn to stop them.**

I'm here

When dealing is complex and the road is difficult for you, ask for help and let it come. It can also be 'just' a prayer. Believe what you ask for is on its way to you. 'Stay' at the checkpoint you discovered quietly, patiently. Reach out to the same pain, to the same voice, to the same inner distress. Tell it "I'm here, all the time," patiently. Heal the inner contraction, hurt, and then love it. Tell it "I'm here."

"I'm here to keep and care, I'm here to have mercy and love, to touch and caress, to feed and order, to teach and direct, I'm here. I take care of everything." Then let go. This will lead to a new movement in your experience, in your body. Maintain your focus and see how your attention works.

Life as well as us, springs naturally

We live with the feeling that we must be active in order for things to happen in our lives. That's true, but it's not an effort. If you think about the process of digestion of food in our body, you will see that we do not have to do anything for this to happen, just do not interfere. **Just** ☺

The body alone knows which substances to absorb into it and which substances it wants to emit out. It always strives for balance; and given the optimal conditions, it does not need our help to arrange itself. We live in an age of advanced medicine and much more will be revealed in the future but no doctor in the world knows how to produce a single blood cell. The body knows.

The same is true with our breath. It just happens. In the same way every other movement in our life happens. Every learning, every renewal, every discovery. We have no way of forcing ourselves to digest, breathe or awaken consciousness. It is difficult for us to grasp this and we will often believe that there is no chance that something will happen if we do not intervene, if we do not make an effort. We have a feeling that we need to make things happen, in order for them to happen. It is so far away from believing in ourselves and from our ability to trust life. Life has its natural spring. It is our job to stop interfering and to enable it.

No one has lived your life before you yet

Fear is the biggest disorder we have. We are afraid to dare because we are afraid to fail or God forbid to succeed, we are afraid to be portrayed in a certain way by others, afraid of what 'they' will say or others will pay a price, afraid.

When you have a vision, an idea or a desire, act. Despite and with the fears and anxieties that arise in you, act. Level through, step by step, **no one has ever lived your life before you and therefore knows nothing about your abilities and capabilities**.

When we stop repairing and improving ourselves and the world and stop interrupting ourselves from being, with all sorts of 'needs and duties' that we think we must do, a creative space becomes available for what we want. We allow ourselves to be and our nature starts to express itself only because we have stopped standing in the way of it.

Who is supposed to approve you?

Many times, we live with an expectation that someone will come and save us, or alternatively come and discover us, put a spotlight on us and then everyone will see the beauty we have as we know it is. The body hurts from waiting. We have a desire and longing to feel accepted, happy and to shine our light. In Hebrew the word 'happy' and the word 'approved' are the exact same word. But who is it that is supposed to confirm us? Who is it that is supposed to discover us? Who is the one that is supposed to illuminate our way?

We feel imprisoned and want to be released. Mostly from the perceptions we hold about life. If you feel that someone is holding your power and deciding for you, it is only because you have given your power away. Take it back.

Our navigation system

Our body is a perfect system - no less - that has the potential to direct our actions if we let it. This is our navigation or guidance system. When we listen to it, we feel good. When we ignore its signs, it exacerbates them. This is true for any situation - mental or physical - in fact they are one. The body comes from life and is constantly in physical reality. Like animals that behave naturally and flow in the world, also the human body in its inherent nature knows how to flow in the world and in the paths of life. In Hebrew the word for animals means 'live.' The animal kingdom is the kingdom of 'live.'

The power of personal history

Many of the beliefs, perceptions, and thoughts that drive our movement in the present are based on past conclusions. I do not underestimate the personal history of anyone, I just want to emphasize that even when the reality of our lives changes and works for us, we tend to revive the past again and again and not pay attention to the new phase, because these beliefs are assimilated within us. This is the way we reconstruct historical conclusions within the realities of our lives.

Our body has its own intelligence

In its nature, the body knows how to live, win, and thrive. Give it the optimal conditions and it will prosper.

When we suffer from pain and serious illness, this is the way the physical system tells us that we are mistaken in 'understanding the material'. Chronicles of pain or anguish, are wake up calls for learning and change. If we want to do better with ourselves, we better explore the triggers that are evoking our pain or anxiety. We better investigate the legality under which the situation arises - what in my behavior creates the situation from which I suffer and what this situation asks of me. We will likely find that one way or another we go against ourselves and respond to the desires, ideas, beliefs, opinions of other people who do not really do good to us.

In our adult lives, it is our responsibility is total for our lifestyle.

The body comes from life and strives to live and be vital as much as possible. It was amazing to see how a dear dog to its owners, whom I know, was run over and underwent surgery. Its hind legs were treated and bandaged, but he could not use them until they recovered. The vet attached it to a two-wheeled fixture so it could move freely. There was not a single morning that this dog woke up upset because of its condition and grumbled about its bitter Fate. On the contrary - very quickly with a first recovery – we were amazed to see how it bounced and was happy as usual; its vitality continued even when it was confined and tied to the fixture.

You will never see an animal waking up in the morning depressed with no desire to start the day. The vitality impulse is so strong that it responds to it immediately, moving in the spaces of existence.

Your body is tuned in for your exclusive benefit

Your body as well - with the emotional sensory systems that exists in it - is constantly in interaction with the world, listening to the body signals as is listening to yourself. It is a system that seeks to flow and knows how to break down barriers that appear along the way. If your stomach tightens during a conversation, ask yourself why this is happening and how to properly relate to this interaction. If you catch a migraine every time you need to talk to the boss, you better check what you can do differently. If you have had shortness of breath for three weeks, you understand that something in the reality of your life is not going your way and it is right to check what it is and how you choose to deal with it for your well-being. This applies to any physical condition. If you understand that your body speaks and directs your behavior and your life constantly in your sole favor, you will stop taking aspirin when your head hurts and Alprazolam when you suffer from an anxiety attack.

Go with or go against

We live out of longing and always want more. The question is whether we flow with life on the way to our next stage or whether oppose it because something scares us. These are the two movements that exist in the universe - go with or go against. Dedication, learning, and inquiry are an expression of belief in self and life, it is 'go with.' To be frozen and not act when we want to is an expression of fear, it is going against.

Our soul loves freedom, it knows infinite spaces, so we always long for freedom but it sounds spoiled and simplistic to us for the most part. We live out of longing. Even in the darkest times I missed 'home' badly, a place I know exists, even if I do not know where it is and could not define it clearly.

In the midst of the listening and responding process we are building a renewed confidence in ourselves. We have come back to trust ourselves, our bodies. As I see it, our body is the 'rock of our existence.' Loyal and truthful.

Even if it looks long, the road back is immediately rewarding as soon as we respond to the pulse.

There is always a way

Home is a warm, loving, protective, throbbing experiential space. When the home is very far away and beats in us so weakly that it is not enough to inspire us to act, to move, the challenge is not to give up. There is a way. There is always a way back home to yourself, to your whole being, a way that rewards you instantly with every step you take toward yourself, towards the source of all things, a way in which we discover all our hidden treasures.

In wars with the inner and outer dragons, we discover courage, focus, strategic thinking, and a fighting spirit. In the swampy swamps of the soul, we discover prayer and faith, inquisitiveness, creativity, initiative, and resourcefulness. In the cracked deserts of emotional neglect, we discover supreme survival, hope, mental strength, determination, and an oasis that provide us with what is necessary for our existence for the time being and more.

Distress is fertile ground for change

Life is not always simple, but it will always provide us with the tools to deal with, when difficulty arises. Sometimes we are caught in a reality that dictates a very limiting belief, we get lost. These are the times when breathing becomes minimal, the anguish is great, the body hurts, but only for signaling us, just so we understand that we are not in the right direction, just so that we can stop the ordinary move and take the action that leads to a relief.

We are here by right and not by grace

We are strong at indescribable levels if we have come this far and it is impossible to describe the abundance that is within our lives right now when even the sky is not the limit.

We are part of an insanely wonderful work that is very difficult to describe in words, called (also) creation. I am in love with being and happy to be a part of this wonderful thing.

It's shaky to realize that we're living here by right and not by grace. We are privileged to be here. It's almost inconceivable. The splendor of creation envelops us, providing everything we need in our journey of development. And there is so much more.

The beauty within which we live

Some time ago we went down to the beach, me, and the girls. The girls raved in the water, the ease with which they ran, raved, laughed, and played, the ease with which they made 3 more new friends to spend an afternoon at the beach with, just like puppies. The utter naturalness in which this happened uplifted me. I looked around at all this mighty beauty that we live in, at all this mighty presence that we do not have to do anything for it to exist. It is there all the time - the shimmering blue sea, the wide beach, the cheers of children. The blue sky, the white clouds that in one moment, a moment of perfection – like, lined up in the sky and stood as symmetrical to the sides of the sun. The splendor of creation. From a distance the fishing rods were visible. In one moment, I was struck by the realization that all this exists and is found without us having to do anything and we are allowed to use and enjoy all this beauty without giving anything in return just take care and not destroy it.

Whether we want it or not, we are all part of this insane,

indescribable beauty, this charming, beautiful azure and white of the clouds and rays of the sun and the sun through the clouds and the waves and all these heads rising up and down in the water, the fishermen in the distance, the rocks, the wind, the people, and the raging children.

Frankly, there is nowhere you should arrive to

There is a phenomenal vitality around us. All our shortages are always full up. It's just the horror stories we tell ourselves in our heads sometimes, that do not allow this abundance within our lives. To be whole is to give everything you are currently experiencing, to be. No judgment holds your focus, your attention, on allowing this magnificent creation which is you, to express itself in the world.

Frankly, there is nowhere you should arrive except being present, embracing all your qualities and abilities that lie within you. To be you, to be within all that you are and not strive to direct anything anywhere really. Let yourself be with all the discomfort, stress, joy, pain, worry, giving, love, hate that arises in order to take you to the next stage of yourself, in order to grow.

I believe that to be whole means to accept ourselves and to know that any pain or distress expresses an area in our experience where we do not allow our love and glow to shine from within.

Free yourself

Sometimes I feel my energy - you might call it love - stuck in my diaphragm or shoulders, face, or knees. I can feel it and so can you. I feel where it's imprisoned and allow 'the prison' –

first of all, to be in my attention. Afterwards, I allow it to open up and let this light that is me, that is you, to shine out between the cracks that get wider gradually. Remember you can go with... and you can go against... both are ok as long as you choose it.

Our growth stems from continuing to, and responding to our potential that seeks to be realized, out of a desire to bring this thing that is 'I,' to be expressed in the world.

Sometimes we are so far away from home, we have lost the way and we cannot find a tip of a thread that will connect us with our life path. It is a dangerous situation and it is important that we remember that there is a way back from it as well. No matter what rock bottom we meet, no matter how far from home we are, there is a way back. There is always a way. These are those times of desiccated cracked emotion deserts, of trauma-scorched soul soil, of minimal breathing.

Always remember that even when the heart is heavy, life awaits you with open arms. We have plenty of air and plenty of opportunities at any given moment. The right to choose whether to participate in this magnificent show of existence is ours.

Because that's how things have always been

That day on the beach it hit me. The show will welcome us with open arms at any given moment and dance with us the dance of our lives as if it has always been like this.

It will never judge us or ask, 'Where have we been for so long' or 'what we were busy with.' It will never deal with the past and will always be satisfied with us and will see the beauty in us, because that is how things have always been.

The Journey Back Home - Hebrew version By Smadar Asraf

המסע חזרה הביתה

והיא קוראת לנו אליה, הבריאה המופלאה. זו קריאה
אינהרנטית, מולדת שקיימת בנו מאז ומעולם. קריאה של
מקום שמעולם לא באמת עזבנו ומעולם לא עזב אותנו, רק
כאילו. אנחנו נמשכים אחריה, כמהים לחוות את כוליות
הרצון – הקיום. להיות אחד עם העולם. המסע הוא הכרתי
להתמזג. לחוות אהבה, להיות אהבה, לחיות. ליהנות.
נפלטנו אל תוך העולם בלידתנו. ההגעה שלנו הנה
טרפה את הקלפים. מצאנו את עצמינו במציאויות חיים
שונות ומגוונות שגם אם הן היו תומכות, הרבה פעמים מבלי
משים , הייחודיות שלנו הופקעה מאיתנו ולפעמים באופן
ברוטלי כשנדרשנו להיענות לתכתיבי המסגרות השונות
שבתוכן גדלנו ובתוכן אנחנו חיות גם היום.
אם להשתמש בדוגמה פשטנית מאוד של מים ושמן, לכל
אחד מהם הטבע שלו. אם נטרוף אותם יחד, נקבל נוזל
לכאורה מעורבב – החיים שלנו על כל ההשפעות
שמשפיעות עלינו, לרוב לא מתוך סינון ובחירה – אבל הטבע
האמיתי של כל אחד מהם נשמר והם מתאחדים אל מקורם

ברגע שמניחים להם להיות. כך הנשמה שלנו, שנטרפה אל תוך מציאות חיים זו או אחרת, אם אנחנו מניחים לה להיות ומזכירים לה את הטבע האמיתי שלה, היא נאספת אל עצמה

ותוך כדי כך הייחודיות המופלאה שלה באה לידי ביטוי בעולם.

געגוע

יש בנו כמיהה אינהרנטית, געגוע, למשהו כמו בלתי מושג שאנחנו יודעים שקיים, משהו נשגב שמאותת לנו על 'מקום' הימצאו, מזמין אותנו אליו ומאיר את מסענו בדרך חזרה הביתה, אליו, אל עצמינו, אל השקט והשלמות של הכוליות חובקת כל שמכילה אותנו בתוכה. שתמיד הכילה.

אפשר להגדיר את ההיענות לכמיהה הזו במושגים ארציים של אהבה, הגשמה עצמית, גילוי עצמי, התפתחות אישית, גדילה. כל אלו הם ורסיות והגדרות שמנסות להסביר במילים אנושיות את הדרך חזרה הביתה, אל עצמנו, שככל שאנחנו צועדות בה אנחנו מרגישות קלות יותר ומרוממות יותר.

כדי לנוע לעבר חוויית גן העדן הזאת, מתוך המציאות הטרופה שרובינו מצויות בה, אנחנו נדרשות למיקוד ולתשומת לב. **אנחנו רוצות ללמוד איך אנחנו מפריעות להוויה הנפלאה הזו שהיא - אנחנו, לבוא לידי ביטוי בעולם ולהפסיק את זה כדי לאפשר לה לפרוח ולהגשם.** בנוסף, אנחנו רוצות לשים לב לכל ה'יש' שכבר קיים בחיינו –

לצד כל עצב מונחת שמחה, לצד כל מחסור מצוי שפע, לצד כל בלבול מצויה בהירות ולצד כל כאב מצויה הקלה. זו תשומת הלב שלנו והבחירה שלנו למה לשים לב שמעצבת את חווויית החיים שלנו. **אנחנו נדרשים להבין מה אנחנו**

רוצים ולאן אנחנו הולכים אבל לא תמיד הדברים ברורים מראש. גם אם הכיוון כללי, תתחילי לצעוד בו, כל השאר יתגלה לך בהמשך. תבטחי.

הדרך מתגלה תוך כדי תנועה

אפשר לדמות את התנועה אל הלא ידוע כנסיעה לעבר מקום לא מוכר. יש במקום הזה נקודה שאת מבקשת להגיע אליה אבל את לא לגמרי יודעת היכן היא ממוקמת. בכל מקרה, את מתחילה לנוע לעברו כשאת יודעת את הכיוון הכללי של הנסיעה. הדרך מתגלה לך תוך כדי תנועה על ידי אינספור רמזים ונקודות ציון. כשאת מגיעה למקום עצמו, כבר הרבה יותר קל לך להיעזר, להתמצא ולהגיע אל היעד הספציפי שאותו את מחפשת.

כך גם בכל מה שנוגע למימוש והגשמה בחיים. את לא תמיד צריכה לדעת איך תכנית ההגשמה העצמית שלך נראית לפרטי פרטים. אם אין לך יעד ספציפי, אלא רק כיוון כללי שעליו את מסכימה, תתחילי לנוע לעברו. הפְּנִיוֹת הספציפיות והפרטים הרלוונטיים יתבהרו לך בהמשך.

אנחנו מניחים שיש מישהו שיודע את התשובות

לרוב, תשומת הלב שלנו מפוזרת. אנחנו לא יודעים מה אנחנו רוצים ולאן אנחנו הולכים בחיים. הרבה פעמים אנחנו בכלל לא יודעים למה אנחנו פה ומה אנחנו עושים פה על הכדור? מי מנהל את העניינים? את מי שואלים? מה הכיוון? מה אמור להנחות את ההתנהגות שלנו? ועוד. אנחנו מניחים שיש מישהו שיודע את התשובות ומתפללים להיתקל בו תוך כדי תנועה, כדי להשתחרר מכל סימני השאלה. זו הסיבה שבגללה אנחנו פונים לדת או למדעים מדויקים, אנחנו מחפשים תשובות. גם הדת וגם הפיזיקה מנסות להבין את היקום, את מקור החומר, מאין באנו, מה פשרנו ולתת מענה לשאלות הקיומיות האלו. הפיזיקה מנסה לעשות את זה גם בלי לערב עניינים של אמונה, גורל, מזל וכולי.

תשומת לב ממוקדת היא מנוע של גילוי והגשמה עצמית

תשומת לב ממוקדת עובדת כמו קרן לייזר. אם תרצי למשל, לקנות מכונית אדומה, פתאום תראי על הכביש הרבה מכוניות אדומות. אם תרצי להיכנס להריון, תגלי שכל אישה שניה פחות או יותר הרה. תשומת לב בשילוב עם הקשבה להדרכה פנימית, הופכת להיות מנוע של גילוי והגשמה עצמית.

להרגיש טוב זו מטרה נעלה, זה לא מותרות

לחישות עדינות' אבל עקשניות ביקשו לכוון את דרכי.' אפשר לקרוא להן רצון, חשק, גחמה, הדרכה או אינטואיציה. למדתי להיענות למה שעושה לי טוב. אישית, ספציפית. הבנתי שיש לי השפעה על איך שאני מרגישה, שזו פונקציה של מה שאני בוחרת – גם אם באופן בלתי מודע – לשים לב אליו. הבנתי שלפעמים אני נמצאת ולפעמים אני נפקדת בתוך חיי, תלוי עם מה אני מתמודדת ועד כמה אני מפחדת ולמדתי שחשוב לשים לב גם לזה, להרחיב את היריעה, לראות תמונה עד כמה שאפשר בשלמותה - רצון מול פחד, אומץ מול תחושה של חוסר שליטה. למדתי שלהרגיש טוב זו מטרה נעלה, שזאת לא בושה. שזה לא מותרות. למדתי שנכון לי לבדוק מה אני רוצה לספוג לתוכי ומה לא, מה אני לוקחת מהחיים ועל מה אני מוותרת ושנכון לדחות את מה שאני לא רוצה גם אם זה הרבה דברים, ושמתוך כל 'מה אני לא', מתבהר לי באורח פלא מה אני כן.

אינטואיציה היא מורה רבת עוצמה

למדתי להקשיב לאינטואיציה, לאותם מסרים שנובעים מתוכי ללא חשיבה רצונית והיענות לה. אינטואיציה היא מורה רבת עוצמה במסענו ההכרתי חזרה הביתה. היא יכולה לעמוד בניגוד לכל רציונל. עיקשת מוזר היה לי להתרחק מחברת נפש של 20 שנים שאהבה

אותי מאוד והייתה יקרה ללבי אבל הרצון להתרחק ולהימנע ממפגש איתה דחק בי. לא יכולתי יותר לאלץ את עצמי לנהוג בניגוד לרצוני ונעניתי לו. לא יכולתי להסביר לעצמי במדויק מה מרתיע אותי עד כדי כך, אבל ידעתי שאני רוצה את המרחק ובסופו של דבר גם התנתקנו. זה הרגיש נכון אז – לפני 10 שנים וזה מרגיש נכון גם היום. היום כבר יש פרספקטיבה, יש בהירות, המניעים לניתוק ברורים למרות שתמיד תהיה לי פינה חמה בלב עבורה. לפעמים דברים שקורים מתבהרים רק בפרספקטיבה של זמן.

אנחנו חייבים ללמוד להימנע מחורים שחורים אנרגטיים ששואבים את האנרגיה שלנו לתוכם במסענו חזרה הביתה, אחרת ניבלע לתוכם, רחוקים שנות אור מהיעד שלנו – לחיות חיים עם משמעות ועניין, חיים מהנים וטובים. קשרים ש'מורידים' אותנו, סופם להסתיים.

השחרור שלנו מכבלי העבר אפשרי וביכולתינו

תשומת הלב שלנו והבחירה איך להשתמש בה מעולם לא היו תלויים בגורם חיצוני. משמע, השחרור שלנו מכבלי העבר, ממסקנות היסטוריות ומאמונות מגבילות הוא אפשרי וביכולתנו. כל תנועה, כל גדילה, נובעים מתוך תשומת לב לפעולה שגויה שלנו והפסקתה. **תשומת לב ומיקוד הם כלים שיש לכייל, לזקק ולאמן לנצח.**

המסע שלנו הוא מסע של היזכרות

תפילה מחברת אותנו עם כוליות הקיום, עם כוח גדול, עם מקור כל הדברים – עם עצמינו. תפילה מאפשרת דיבור ישיר בלתי אמצעי עם האינטליגנציה חובקת כל שאנחנו חלק ממנה. המסע שלנו על פני הכדור הוא מסע של היזכרות במהות האמיתית שלנו. כל מה שנחוץ למסע מצוי כבר בתוכנו ובהישג ידינו.

הבית – האמיתי – פועם בתוכנו

בית זה לא רק מקום, בית זה חוויה. בית זה חום, ביטחון

והגנה. לפעמים זיכרון הבית שלנו חלוש ורחוק כי התנסויות החיים שלנו היו קשות ומאתגרות עד מאוד ואולי הן עדיין **אבל גם מהמרחקים, הבית – האמתי – פועם בתוכנו, חי וקיים, שולח פולסים של חיות, מאותת לנו איזו דרך נכון לנו לקחת, עם מי נכון לדבר ומה נכון לעשות בדרך אליו.** פיתוח הקשבה להדרכה ולאינטואיציה שמגיעות מפנים ההוויה שלנו היא קריטית למסע. היא מאפשרת לנו להיענות לקריאה הזאת ולפתח מערכת של יחסי אמון בתוך עצמינו ועם החיים.

כאב הוא בן ברית

כאב הוא חלק בלתי נפרד מהקיום שלנו. כאב הוא בן ברית. פניו לשלום תמיד. הוא לא אישי, יש לו תפקיד - הוא מסמן גבול. הוא מסמן בגוף ובנפש השפעות של אי סדרים בתפיסת העולם, פחדים ואמונות מגבילות, ש'לאורן' אנחנו חיים. לפעמים כאב הוא ביטוי של פצע חי ואמיתי. בכל מקרה הוא קיים כדי לעורר אותנו, דורש תשומת לב וחקירה. אדם שגדל בבית שבו מלא באלימות והגיב שוב ושוב בהתכנסות הגוף כדי לא לחטוף, יצא לחיים עצמאיים עם ראש שפוף, לפעמים סובל ממגרנות וכאבי כתפיים שהתאבנבו בגלל שנים של אימון בסגירות. לפעמים יסבול מדבר אחר. אותו כאב מספר לו שהוא עושה משהו שגוי בהחזקת הגוף שלו ובגדול, מבקש ממנו למצוא את הדרך להזדקף שוב מול החיים.

חזון חיים מושך אותנו אליו

אל מול יחסי השלום שאנחנו מפתחות עם כאב, כדאי שיהיה לנו חזון חיים גם אם הוא כללי מאוד, גם אם הוא רק חוויתי. כשרציתי זוגיות בגיל מאוחר, זו היתה רק הידיעה של - איך אני רוצה להרגיש במערכת היחסים הבאה שלי, ברשימה item שהחזיקתי בתשומת הלב שלי. ויתרתי על כל שניסתה לתאר את מי שאמור להיות בן הזוג שלי והתמקדתי

בתחושה שאני מזמנת אל תוך חיי כשיופיע האדם הזה.
התמקדתי ב – איך ירגיש ה'ביחד' שלנו.

אם הייתי מחזיקה את כל אותן אמונות של מי אמור
להיות האיש, לא היינו יחד היום. אני מאמינה שמשכתי אל
תוך חיי אהבה כל כך יפה בגיל 46 כי התמקדתי בחזון שהיה
לי על מערכת יחסים - ברור היה לי איך אני רוצה להרגיש
בתוך הקשר, אחרת אין לי אפשרות להסביר איך התחברתי
עם אדם שרחוק ממני שנות אור בכל כך הרבה דברים אבל
שותף לגן העדן שיצרנו.

גם את האמונות הכי מגבילות שלנו אפשר לשנות

כוחן של אמונות מגבילות הוא חזק ועוצמתי. לפעמים
הצלחנו להשתכנע שכזכה הם פני הדברים באמת, שאם אני
חיה בחוויית מחסור מתוך אמונה ש"לעולם לא יהיה לי
מספיק כסף", כנראה שכזכה זה יהיה גם בעתיד. שלמרות
שאני רוצה מאוד בן זוג, אני מאמינה ש"לא מגיע לי" ולכן זה
לא הולך לקרות. אבל גם את האמונות המגבילות ביותר
שלנו אפשר למוסס, לפרק ולפתח במקומן אמונות וחוויות
רגשיות חדשות וטובות. בשביל זה נשתמש בחקירה,
ובתשומת לב. כשקשה לך תבדקי איפה בגוף הנפלא והחכם
שלך את מתוחה כרגע? איפה כואב לך? גם הכאב הכי קטן
הוא קצה חוט חזרה פנימה אל תוך חוויית הכוליות.

הגוף מנסה לספר לך משהו

התמקדות ותשומת לב לכאב והסכמה לחוות ולאפשר
אותו, להאיר עליו לרגע במקום לברוח ממנו או לנסות
להיפטר ממנו, יוצרת בו שינוי. נכון לתת לכאב מקום ולנסות
להבין למה הוא כאן ומה הוא בעצם מבקש? את רוצה
להרגיש אחרת, **את פורצת דרך**. אבל לפני יציאה למחוז
חוויה חדש, נכון לתת למה שיש כרגע להיות, גם אם זה כואב.

אני כאן

כשהתתמודדות מורכבת והדרך קשה לך, תבקשי עזרה

ותני לה להגיע. זו יכולה להיות גם 'רק' תפילה. תאמיני שהיא
בדרך אלייך. 'תשהי' במחסום שגילית בשקט, בסבלנות.
תושיטי יד לאותו הכאב, לאותו הקול, לאותה מועקה
פנימית. תגידי להם "**אני כאן כל זמן שצריך**", בסבלנות.
תרפי את הכיווץ הפנימי, תכאבי, תאהבי. תגידי לו "אני כאן".
"אני כאן כדי לשמור ולטפל, אני כאן כדי לחמול ולאהוב, כדי
לגעת וללטף, כדי להאכיל ולסדר, כדי ללמד ולכוון, אני כאן.
מטפלת בכל". תרפי. זה יוביל תנועה חדשה בחוויה שלך,
בגוף שלך. תשמרי על מיקוד ותראי איך תשומת הלב שלך
עובדת.

לחיים כמו גם לנו, יש נביעה טבעית

אנחנו חיים בתחושה שאנחנו חייבים להיות אקטיביים על
מנת שדברים יקרו בחיים שלנו. זה נכון, אבל זה לא מאמץ.
אם תחשבי על תהליך העיכול של המזון בגופנו, תראי
שאנחנו לא צריכים לעשות שום דבר על מנת שזה יקרה, רק
לא להפריע. כך גם כשאנחנו נושמים. באותו האופן קורית
כל תנועה אחרת בחיים שלנו. כל למידה, כל התחדשות, כל
יצירה מגיעים כנביעה פנימית, אם לא נפריע לעצמינו להיות.
אין לנו דרך לכפות על עצמינו עיכול, נשימה או התעוררות
רוחנית. אנחנו מאמינים שאנחנו צריכים לגרום לדברים
לקרות, על מנת שיקרו אבל בעצם כשאנחנו פועלים מתוך
תשומת לב לעצמינו גם כחלק מהסביבה שבתוכה אנחנו
חיים, אנחנו מוצאים שכמו לחיים, גם לנו, יש נביעה טבעית.
"העבודה" שלנו היא להפסיק להפריע לה ולאפשר אותה.

אף אחד עוד לא חי את החיים שלך לפנייך

פחד הוא ההפרעה הכי גדולה שיש לנו. אנחנו מפחדים
להעז כי אנחנו מפחדים להיכשל או חלילה להצליח, אנחנו
מפחדים להצטייר באופן מסוים על ידי אחרים, מפחדים
ממה יגידו או שאחרים ישלמו מחיר, מפחדים..
כשיש לך חזון, רעיון או רצון, תפעלי. למרות ועם

החששות והפחדים שמתעוררים בך, תפעלי. תפלסי דרך, תצעדי צעד צעד, **אף אחד עוד לא חי את החיים שלך לפנייך ולכן לא יודע דבר על היכולות והמסוגלויות שלך.**

כשאנחנו מפסיקים לתקן ולשפר את עצמינו ואת העולם ומפסיקים להפריע לעצמינו להיות, עם כל מיני 'צריכ'ים וחובות שנדמה לנו שאנחנו חייבות לעשות, מתפנה מרחב יצירה למה שאנחנו רוצות. אנחנו מאפשרות לעצמינו להיות ולטבע שלנו להתחיל לבטא את עצמו רק כי הפסקנו לעמוד בדרך.

מי אמור לאשר אותך?

הרבה פעמים אנחנו חיות בציפייה שמישהו יבוא ויציל אותנו, או לחילופין יבוא ויגלה אותנו, יאיר עלינו עם אורות במה ואז כולם יראו את היופי שיש בנו כמו שאנחנו יודעות שהוא. הגוף כואב מהַהַמְתָּנָה. יש בנו רצון וכמיהה לקבל הכרה, קבלה, להיות מאושרות ולהאיר את אורינו. המילה (happy). וגם שמחה (approved) מאושר מבטאת גם אישור אבל מי הוא זה שאמור לאשר? מי הוא זה שאמור לגלות? מי הוא זה שאמור להאיר אותך אם לא את מבפנים החוצה? אם את מרגישה כלואה ומבקשת להשתחרר זה רק בגלל שאת לא סומכת על עצמך שתמצאי את הדרך הנכונה עבורך כשתעזי לעשות צעד. הרבה פעמים אנחנו נצמדים למוכר והידוע שעם זאת שהוא בטוח ומגונן, הוא גם רדום ומשעמם.

החופש שאנחנו מבקשות הוא בעיקר חופש מתפיסות שאנחנו מחזיקות בהן לגבי החיים שגורמות לנו להרגיש פחד, מחוייבות, אשמה, מצפון... השלימי את החסר אם את מרגישה שמישהו מחזיק בכוח שלך ומחליט עבורך, זה רק בגלל שאת הענקת לו את הכוח הזה. קחי אותו חזרה.

מערכת הניווט שלנו

הגוף שלנו הוא מערכת מושלמת – לא פחות – שמכוונת את פעולותינו. זו מערכת הניווט שלנו. כשאנחנו מקשיבים לה, אנחנו מרגישים טוב. כשאנחנו מתעלמים מאותותיה, היא מחריפה אותם. זה נכון לגבי כל מצב – נפשי או פיזי – כשלמעשה הם אחד. הגוף בא מן החיים ומצוי במציאות תמיד. כמו חיות שמתנהלות בטבעיות ובזרימה בעולם, כך גם גוף האדם בטבע שלו יודע זרימה בעולם ובנתיבי החיים, מהי. **חשבת פעם למה קוראים לחיות חיות? הן חיות, תכלס, ב'כאן ועכשיו'. ממלכת החי בטבע היא ממלכה נוכחת.**

כוחה של היסטוריה אישית

הרבה מהאמונות, התפיסות, והמחשבות שמנהלות את התנועה שלנו בהווה מבוסס על מסקנות עבר. אני לא מזלזלת חלילה בהיסטוריה האישית של אף אדם רק מבקשת להדגיש שגם כשמציאות החיים שלנו משתנה לטובה, אנחנו נוטים להחיות את העבר שוב ושוב ולשכוח מהקיום שלנו בנוכחות, כי זה מה שנטמע בנו. אנחנו אלופים בשחזור מסקנות היסטוריות בתוך מציאות החיים שלנו.

הגוף שלנו חכם

בטבע שלו, הגוף יודע איך לחיות ולנצח שואף לאיזון. לא צריך להגיד לו איך לחיות, זה בטבע שלו. כשאנחנו סובלים מכאובים ומחלות קשות, זו הדרך של המערכת הגופנית לומר לנו שאנחנו שוגים ב'הבנת המטריה'. כרוניקה של כאב או תעוקה, הם קריאה ללמידה ולשינוי. אם ברצוננו להיטיב עם עצמנו, כדאי שנחקור את הטריגרים שעוררו את אותו הכאב, תעוקה או חרדה. כדאי שנחקור את החוקיות של המצב – מה בהתנהגות שלי יוצר את המצב שממנו אני סובלת ומה הוא מבקש ממני. סביר להניח שנגלה שבדרך זו או אחרת אנחנו הולכים נגד עצמינו ונענים לרצונות,

רעיונות, אמונות, דעות של אנשים אחרים שלא באמת מיטיבים איתנו. בחיינו הבוגרים האחריות שלנו על אורחות חיינו, היא שלנו והיא מלאה.

הגוף בא מן החיים ושואף לחיות מקסימלית, תמיד אזכור את הסיפור על הכלבה הזו, שהיתה אהובה ויקרה לבעליה, שנדרסה ועברה ניתוח. הרגליים האחוריות טופלו ונחבשו אבל היא לא יכולה היתה להשתמש בהן עד שיחלימו. חיברו אותה למתקן עם שני גלגלים אחוריים כדי שתוכל לנוע בחופשיות. לא היה בוקר אחד שהכלבה הזאת התעוררה מצוברחת בבוקר בגלל מצבה וקיטרה על מר גורלה, להיפך – מהר מאוד עם התאוששות ראשונה מדהים היה לראות איך היא מקפצת ושמחה כהרגלה ונשארה חיונית גם כשהיתה מוגבלת וקשורה למתקן.

את לעולם לא תראי בעל חיים שמתעורר בבוקר מדופרס בלי חשק להתחיל את היום. דחף החיות חזק בו יותר מכל והוא נענה לו, נע במרחבי הקיום.

הגוף שלך מכוון לטובתך הבלעדית

גם הגוף שלך על המערכת הרגשית, תחושתית שקיימת בו, מצוי תמידית באינטראקציה עם העולם. להקשיב לגוף זה בעצם להקשיב לעצמך. הגוף הוא מערכת שמבקשת לזרום ויודעת לפרק חסמים שמופיעים בה. אם מתכווצת לך הבטן תוך כדי שיחה, תשאלי את עצמך למה זה קורה ואיך נכון לך להתייחס באינטראקציה הזאת. אם את חוטפת מגרנה בכל פעם שאת צריכה לדבר עם הבוס, כדאי שתבדקי ממה את בורחת ולמה את כל כך מפחדת. אם יש לך קוצר נשימה כבר שלושה שבועות, תביני שמשהו במציאות החיים שלך לא מתנהל לרוחך ונכון שתבדקי מה הדבר ואיך את בוחרת להתמודד איתו לרווחתך. הדברים תקפים לכל מצב גופני. אם תביני שהגוף שלך מדבר ומכוון לטובתך הבלעדית, את constantly את התנהגותך וחייך

תפסיקי לקחת אספירין כשכואב לך הראש וקסנאקס כשאת סובלת מהתקף חרדה.

ללכת עם או ללכת נגד

אנחנו חיים מתוך כמיהה ותמיד רוצים עוד. השאלה היא האם אנחנו זורמים עם החיים בדרך לשלב הבא שלנו או מתנגדים להם כי משהו מפחיד אותנו. אלו הן שתי התנועות שקיימות ביקום - ללכת עם או ללכת נגד. התמסרות, למידה וחקירה הן ביטוי של אמונה בעצמי ובחיים, זה ללכת עם. קפיאה במקום היא ביטוי של פחד, זה ללכת נגד.

אנחנו אוהבים חופש וכמהים לחופש תמיד אבל זה נשמע לנו מפונק ופשטני לרוב. עם זאת, אני מזמינה אותך לפרגן לעצמך יותר רגעים של חופש, פינוק והנאה שבהן את עושה את מה שאת רוצה באמת. אני בטוחה שהקשבה למה שאת רוצה והיענות לה גם בדברים הקטנים, תגביר את תחושת ההנאה שלך ותוביל אותך בסופו של דבר לגילוי עצמי.

בעיצומו של תהליך הקשבה והיענות לרצון האמיתי שלנו, אנחנו בונות אמון מחודש וחוזרות לסמוך על עצמינו.

חוזרות הביתה. תמיד תזכרי שגם כשהדרך נראית לך ארוכה, היא מתגמלת מיידית ברגע שאת מבינה מה הרצון שלך ונענית לו.

תמיד יש דרך

הווית הבית היא כמו מרחב חוויתי חם, אוהב, מגן, פועם. כשהבית רחוק מאוד והפעימה שלו בנו היא כל כך חלשה שזה לא מספיק כדי לעורר אותנו לפעולה, לתנועה, האתגר הוא לא לוותר. יש דרך. **תמיד יש דרך חזרה הביתה אל עצמך**, אל כוליותך, דרך שמתגמלת אותך מיידית עם כל צעד שאת עושה אלייך, אל מקור כל הדברים', דרך שאנחנו מגלים בה את כל האוצרות החבויים שלנו.

במלחמות עם הדרקונים הפנימיים והחיצוניים אנחנו

מגלים אומץ, עוז, חשיבה אסטרטגית ורוח לחימה. בביצות הטובעניות של הנפש אנחנו מגלים תפילה ואמונה, חקירה, יצירתיות, יוזמה ותושייה. במדבריות הרגש הסדוקות מיובש והזנחה אנחנו מגלים שרידה עילאית, תקווה, תעצומות נפש, נחישות, ונווה מדבריות שמספקים לנו את הנחוץ לקיומנו להמשך המסע.

מצוקה היא קרקע פוריה לשינוי

החיים לא תמיד פשוטים, אבל תמיד יספקו לנו גם את הכלים להתמודדות במקומות שבהם מופיע קושי. לפעמים אנחנו נתפסים למציאות שמוכתבת על ידי אמונה מגבילה מאוד, הולכים לאיבוד בדרך למקום שאנחנו לא רוצים להגיע אליו.. אלו הזמנים שבהם הנשימה נעשית מינימאלית, התעוקה גדולה, הגוף כואב, אבל רק כדי לאותת לנו, רק כדי שנבין שאנחנו לא בכיוון הנכון, רק כדי שנעצור את המהלך הרגיל ונעשה את הפעולה שמובילה להקלה.

אנחנו פה בזכות ולא בחסד

אנחנו חזקים ברמות שלא ניתנות לתיאור אם הגענו עד כאן ואי אפשר להתחיל לתאר את השפע שנמצא בתוך החיים שלנו כבר עכשיו כשאפילו השמיים הם לא הגבול. אנחנו חלק מיצירה מופלאה, קשה לתאר אותה במילים. אני מאוהבת בהוויה הזאת שנקראת (גם) בריאה ומאושרת להיות חלק ממנה ולהתקיים בתוכו.

זה מטלטל לקלוט שאנחנו חיים פה על הכדור, בזכות. יש לנו הזכות להיות פה. זה בלתי נתפס כמעט איך כל העולם הזה פרוס לרגלינו. פאר היצירה עוטף אותנו ומספק לנו את כל מה שאנחנו זקוקים לו לאורך הדרך וכמה הרבה יש.

היופי שבתוכו אנחנו חיים

לפני זמן מה ירדנו לים, הבנות השתוללו במים, הקלות שבה הן רצות, משתוללות, צוחקות ומשחקות, הקלות שבה הן עשו עוד 3 חברות חדשות לבילוי של אחר צהריים בחוף,

כמו גורות. הטבעיות הגמורה שבה זה קרה.. הסתכלתי
מסביב על כל ה'יש' האדיר הזה שאנחנו חיים בתוכו. כל
ה'יש' האדיר הזה שאנחנו לא צריכים לעשות כלום כדי שהוא
יתקיים, הוא שם כל הזמן –
הים הכחול המנצנץ,
החוף הרחב,
צהלות ילדים.
השמיים התכולים,
העננים הלבנים שברגע אחד, רגע של שלמות – הסתדרו
בשמיים ועמדו כמו סימטריים לצידי השמש - פאר היצירה.
מרחוק נראו חכות הדייגים..
ברגע אחד היכתה בי ההכרה - כל זה קיים ונמצא בלי
שנצטרך לעשות דבר ואנחנו רשאים להשתמש וליהנות מכל
היופי הזה בלי לתת דבר בתמורה מלבד לשמור עליו.
אם נרצה או לא נרצה כולנו חלק מהיופי האינסופי הזה,
הבלתי ניתן לתיאור הזה, התכלת היפהיפיה הזאת והלבן של
העננים והקרניים של השמש והשמש מבעד לעננים והגלים
וכל הראשים האלה שעולים ויורדים בתוך המים והדייגים
והסלעים וכל האנשים והרוח והילדים המשתוללים..

תכלס, אין לאן להגיע

יש חיות פנומנאלית סביבינו. כל מחסורינו מלא תמיד. זה
רק סיפורי הזוועה שאנחנו מספרים לעצמינו בראש כל
הזמן, שלא מאפשרים את הטוב הזה בתוך החיים שלנו.
להיות שלמה זה לתת לכל מה שאת חווה כרגע, להיות.
בלי שיפוטיות, בלי רצון לגמור עם זה כבר עם נאמנות
מקסימלית לעצמך. לתת לכל מה שיש להיות ולשמור על
מיקוד שמציין עבורך לאן את נעה במסער. תכלס, אין לאן
להגיע חוץ מאשר להסתנכרן עם **הנוכחות המלאה שלך,**
על כל האיכויות והיכולות שטמונים בך כאדם. להיות את,
לשהות בתוך כל מה שהוא את ולא להתאמץ לכוון שום דבר

לשום מקום. **לעשות את מה שאת מאמינה שאת צריכה לעשות** ולאפשר לעצמך לחוות את הכל - כל חוסר נוחות, מתח, שמחה, כאב, דאגה, נתינה, אהבה, שנאה שמתעוררים בך כדי לקחת אותך לשלב הבא של עצמך, לגדילה.

לשחרר את עצמך לחופשי

לפעמים אני מרגישה את שמשהו תקוע לי בסרעפת או בכתפיים, בפנים או בברכיים, אני מרגישה אנרגיה עומדת, תפוסה. אני מרגישה איפה היא כלואה ולפעמים כולאת אותה יותר. בכוח, ואז מרפה, מאפשרת לכלא הזה להיפתח ולתת לחיות שיש במקום לזרוח החוצה בין הסדקים. זה מרחיב אותם ועוזר להם להיפתח.

להיות שלמה מבחינתי זה לחיות את עצמך עד הסוף ולדעת שכל כאב או מועקה מבטאים עוד מקום בחוויה שלך או בגוף שלך שבהם את לא מאפשרת אהבה. להיות שלמה זה להפסיק להילחם בעצמך ולבחור בזרימה ואז בהדרגה היא מרככת אותך ופותחת כל מחסום.

הגדילה שלנו נובעת ממשיכה אל, והיענות לפוטנציאל שלנו שמבקש להתממש, מתוך רצון להביא את הדבר הזה שהוא 'אני', לידי ביטוי בעולם.

לפעמים כל כך התרחקנו מהבית, איבדנו את הדרך ואנחנו לא מצליחים למצוא קצה חוט שיחבר אותנו עם נתיב החיים שלנו, זה מצב מסוכן וחשוב שנזכור שגם ממנו יש דרך חזרה. לא משנה באיזו נקודת שפל אנחנו נמצאים, לא משנה כמה רחוק מהבית אנחנו, יש דרך חזרה אליו. תמיד יש דרך. אלו אותם זמנים של מדבריות רגש סדוקות מיובש, של אדמת נפש חרוכה מטראומה, של נשימה מינימלית. תמיד תזכרי שגם כשהלב כבד החיים מחכים לך בזרועות פתוחות.

יש לנו אויר בשפע ושפע הזדמנויות בכל רגע נתון. זכות הבחירה אם להשתתף במופע הזה של הקיום היא שלנו.

כי ככה היו הדברים מאז ומעולם

באותו היום על החוף זה היכה בי, המופע מקבל אותנו בזרועות פתוחות בכל רגע נתון ויר קוד איתנו את ריקוד חיינו כאילו זה היה ככה מאז ומעולם. לעולם לא ישפוט אותנו על – 'איפה היינו עד היום' ובמה היינו עסוקים כשפספסנו את ההוויה, לעולם לא יתעסק בעבר ותמיד נמצא ויהיה בשביעות רצון ובאהבה, יראה את היופי, כי ככה היו הדברים מאז ומעולם

Acknowledgments

No book is created all on its own. This book is certainly not an exception.

The "Sisterhood" – we came together and supported each other. Judy, Heidi, Dani, Maria, Yve, Kerri, Smadar, and Manjusri took a leap of faith and discomfort to step into my questions as to whether we could create a book. We spent months of preparation as Dani would lead us in mini-inspirational writing times on our weekly calls. The idea of taking a word and creating a fictional piece or a non-fictional piece came to life. To step out of all of our comfort zones, we chose to use fiction as the basis, with Smadar's story anchoring us at the end into actions. There is a truth in many fiction stories as authors write them. Some are more closely aligned with who they are in the moment, or a lesson that is being learned in that moment. The emotions and feelings for the author are real as they write at the very least, even if the situation is very different than reality.

Each moment and each step of this book met resistance as we worked through our stories in our own way. Beautiful resistance that helped us each grow and show us more of our own path than before.

I have several other "sister circles" that helped me progress to this point where I had visions and nudges when I asked for help and sometimes when I didn't. The first is the SiStars – Julie Ann, Arti, Leslie, and Kate. We worked through business ideas as a small mastermind group. Another group formed through a course I took – Adina, Anastasia, Anna, Brittany, Cara, Gail, Gozi, and Juliette. In both of these circles, while the focus was business building, I learned from each of these women in so many ways.

Then came my Gateless sister circle – a writing circle that allowed me to share my "glitter unicorn poop" stories with them every week for months. A step back into a form of writing that I embraced for the first time. Thank you Kittie, Kim, Shawn, Becky, Cathy and Tammy. Your stories made my life richer as we found spaces to heal ourselves through our stories.

I also will say thank you to an amazing group of individuals who listened to me say that I would be a publisher in my October 2018 Lifebook vision – Sandra, Missy, Jennifer, Scott, Manex, John, Jolaine, Bridget, Bob, Andriana, Maria, Alan, Myya, Cheryl, Trish and Spencer. In that lovely dark chocolate cocoon, enjoying Purity Coffee, you gave me visions of other options, other ways of doing things. For this I will always be blessed beyond a mere thank you.

My loving family and friends, who live near and far, also have heard my vision. I thank all of them for the support and patience as I grew into creating this book. And I especially thank my children and fur baby, who have allowed me to create and be over the last year. They also required a great deal of patience while I had my head into editing and some times, they needed to handle dinner creation as I lost track of time.

One of my lovely children created the cover art for this book.

This book represents a new part of my life journey - one of supporting those who want to write, who have a story to tell, and believe they can't.

Our advanced readers provided beautiful messages and comments that allowed us to enhance our stories. We thank you for every comment.

Many thanks to those who have purchased this book. We hope that the stories speak to you and carry you through to a new thought in your life. Or perhaps a reminder of a thought that existed long ago and needed to be uncovered.

May there be blessings abounding to all.

~ Kathryn

About the Authors

Manjusri Nair is a Surgeon, Yoga practitioner, and an avid reader. A wife and a mother, Manjusri writes poetry, fiction, and non-fiction born out of meditativeness and a sense of offering. She lives in Mumbai, India.

You can read more of her writings at https://itstimeto.co.uk

***

Dani Glaeser is a writer, poet, artist, explorer, occasional muse, and so much more with a propensity for writing poetry, in particular haikus, as well as abundant alliteration. She's a Certified Lifebook Leader who enjoys living the Lifebook Lifestyle, creating empowering and inspirational experiences, and spaces to breathe.

When she isn't playfully fitting a life experience into a haiku or other form of poetry, she enjoys capturing life's moments in words, asking hard questions, or creating fictional short stories (like the one above). She knows writing and art can be powerful tools to connect us to those inner voices that we tend to ignore, but really benefit us when we listen to them, as well as enable us to explore ideas and visions via play, and that gratitude, appreciation, and mindset can make all the difference.

At the age of 8, Dani's Aunt Les discovered her writing journal, and framed one of her poems. Writing has always been a part of her life as she pretended to write before she knew how to form letters, transferred emotions and moments into poetry, even her degree reflects her love of writing. Rarely does a day pass when she has not written something. She even incorporates writing into her retreats and workshops as well as creative mapping and intuitive meditations.

When she is not writing, you can find her with her family (Sunday mornings she plays Bananagrams with her beloved hubby), out for a walk, meditating, cozied up with a good book, or creating spaces of grace in the form of mini retreats/ refuges from the chaos of today's world. She is a practitioner of gratitude and compassion, lifelong learner, seeker of understanding, lover of tea, and promoter of self-care.

To find out more about Dani, you can find her hanging out here: https://innerlighthousemusings.com/ and on Instagram @innerlighthousemusings

She shares her haikus and life moments here: https://www.instagram.com/beingalighthouse/

She also hangs out with 8 other wonderful women here: https://itstimeto.co.uk

(Where you can find a few of her intuitive meditations and more.)

***

Kate Heartwright is the pen name for Kathryn Cart-wright.

Kathryn is a developmental content editor and a four-time Amazon bestselling author. She firmly maintains that the original voice of the storyteller is one of the most important parts of publishing. She also believes that everyone is a storyteller. Whether fiction, non-fiction, or technical manuals, all writing tells a story with the right content. Kathryn started exploring developmental editing early in life. Her belief was that it would have been better to turn all the bad witches into good by loving them. Kathryn continues to share the love through her focus on developmental editing which allows authors to create stories that resonate with the world.

With having children, and actively volunteering with Girl Scouts, Mindvalley and The Lifebook Company, LLC, Kathryn's passion of learning and interesting conversations over a cup of coffee with friends with wide ranging topics bring her happiness.

When Kathryn is not editing, she is likely to have her nose

in a book, a kitten on her lap, and a cup of coffee or tea in her hand, soaking up the warm sunshine on the couch and enjoying a few minutes of peace. Once a year, she takes an unplugged vacation to a cabin with a beautiful lake, surrounded by pine trees and blueberry bushes, where cell phone signals are almost non-existent for a "being break" from the rest of the world.

You can find her at: www.writeeditshare.com (as an editor) and www.writeadream.life (as an author) as well as at https://www.itstimeto.co.uk

***

Maria Kostelac – Creative Communicator dedicated to the elevation of technology in service of the planet and society. Her thought-leadership business serves this - her guiding mission - through the roles she plays as management consultant, entrepreneur, executive & career coach, writer, public speaker, and corporate activist. Her work, a two-decade testimony to her conviction that life is art, serves to transform well hewn business mindsets and conventions of our time into a celebration of humility, trust, joy, and the sacred beauty of the world we inhabit.

The merging of technology, business, life, art, commerce, and self is explored through her writings as columnist, blogger, corporate copywriter, and change agent. She explores the multifaceted means of creating worlds of ease, splendour, delight, comedy, conversation, ritual, connection, abundance, covenant, and adoration through the practice of profession.

While her career as management consultant and best-practice

educator affords her expanded access to the realms of business leaders, her passion pivots off her roots in theatre, art, philosophy, literature, and music: To inspire the next generation of leaders, innovators, and game-changers toward the societal and philosophical consequences their contributions might serve to influence and explore.

In Memorare, Maria dedicates her own tender self-reflection to women, the world over, who are striving to fulfill the roles they hold in society as nurturers, partners, professionals, and pioneers may have eclipsed their hearts' deepest longing and seeking. It is a sacred pause from the endless striving "towards" ... An offering of reverent review.

***

Kerri Beth Overington is a multidisciplinary designer creating residences, professional spaces, textiles, and events worldwide. Her designs are harmonic, connecting inhabitant with the living space, and environment. Intrigued by designing the walls, as much as she is by the stories they tell, she approaches design holistically creating objects derived from the earth and crafted to be enjoyed in daily life and festivity for generations.

She offers perspective and practicum to embody happiness through a conscious lifestyle. Her writing and exploration through world travel, creative process, continued education, working with clients worldwide, and volunteering with youth and community housing inspires her to continually metamorphosis to the next layer of development.

***

Judy Loe is a proud mother of two adult children. As a Transformational Coach in Health and Wellness, she is dedicated to helping women regain their health, vitality, and radiance. She is also a Certified Lifebook Leader guiding those who have committed to turning their life into a masterpiece. She is currently traveling ...excited to make the best of her next phase in life.

You can find Judy at www.thrivewithjudy.com

***

Heidi Tyler medically retired at the age of 54 and went on to become an author, emotional intelligence coach, certified belief clearing coach, certified Lifebook Leader, founder of https://itstimeto.co.uk and co-founder of https://www.facebook.com/InnerFreedomOuterVision/

Heidi's vision is to help 000's of people around the world live their best life.

Heidi was a former project, programme, quality and people manager in a corporate environment which crafted her expertise in creating and achieving goals while at the same time building great relationships with her global team. Heidi knew she needed to rebuild her own life after her early retirement and through exploring personal development at a far greater depth she quite literally transformed her life. Through the knowledge she had gained from her former career, overcoming all of her medical conditions and her love of her newfound learning, she realised she had the ability to help others create and achieve their own goals, by focusing on what's holding them back. Whether it's beliefs, values, habits, emotions, the big WHY (Purpose), goal setting or needing to be held accountable, Heidi moves people forward to a new journey of empowerment and success.

Heidi has not stood still with growth and development and continues to look at other areas where she can expand her knowledge and skillset.

Heidi loves to explore alternative ways of looking at life, most notably Karmic astrology, which led to the creation of Nixie. In her spare time she simply adores spending time having fun with her family, reading and creating new ideas and projects.

If you'd love to move forward into your new journey, contact Heidi through her website https://itsyourtimeto.co.uk

***

Yvette Simpson - 18 years ago it seemed like I had it all – business success, married with incredible children, family and friends, amazing holidays, and lifestyle– a blessed life! Many people later told me "You looked like you had a perfect life."

However, the reality was it did not feel perfect. I constantly had this nagging feeling that something was not quite right inside my own Soul, something was missing but I just could not figure it out - it did not make sense. I had achieved so much in my life; I got my primary degree and my Master's degree in business. I had married the supposed love of my life and we had set up two successful companies and we developed a wonderful lifestyle for ourselves. Yet still, I had this deep lack of fulfillment that I longed to fix.

In 1996 I started down the road of personal development. I read every personal development guru book I could find, I hired a coach, I learned Reiki, Integrated Energy Therapy, Neuro-Linguistic Programming, Holistic Health, Crystals, Wiccan, various forms of Meditation - I literally could go on and on but you get the idea.

Everything I learned just kept leading to diving into another course. And yet, the emptiness "thing" stayed within me.

I began to notice that after years and years, sure I had completed a ton of self-help modules but I wasn't closing the gap inside. I found myself in a revolving door of personal development programs because deep inside I knew there was a truth I needed to find.

I began examining and documenting how people all around me were reacting to minor daily challenges, triggers points, breaking points, and non-negotiables. I examined my own reactions to these things and I researched and explored Shadow Work. In short, I built a "Soul Search Tool-Kit" for transforming every aspect of my daily life. I learned how to be truly, deeply, and personally at peace within my own Soul. Furthermore, I have learned how to use the tools to enhance all of the relationships I choose to be part of.

I can finally say I LIVE joyfully each and every day. I have more clarity than I've ever had and best of all it led me to discover my own Life Mission.

***

Smadar Asraf - At the age of 24, I was confused, lost if you will, and was exposed to the Grinberg Method. I realized it worked. I did not know exactly how, so I decided to study the method in a 3-year track. Who would have believed that I started my professional path at that moment, about 26 years ago?

During those years, I've learned various courses and went through various pieces of training in Europe and the US, I have learned and experimented with ways of diving inward and studying the self.

At the age of 44, after 20 years of working with people in a thriving clinic, I left Tel Aviv and set out on a journey whose purpose was love - to find the man with whom I want to share my life with. Today, into the fifth year within the paradise we have created, I can say that this journey was - the heart's journey.

I believe that all our dreams and goals are within our reach and that our job is to stop interfering and recall our true nature that knows how to flow in the paths of life, towards them. This is what I do in my own life and this is what I pass on to the people I come in contact with. It all begins and ends within us.

***

Our Souls are filled with Love.

Also By

Also By

Heidi C. Tyler
A Mixture of Feelings
Kathryn Cartwright - contributing author to:
Calling All Earth Angels and Healers
The Untethered Woman
Wild Women Rising
Life is A Gift: Loving You
Mother, Self Queen
Dr. Manjusri Nair - published poems:
Soul Hymns
Emanation
All the Authors blog at:
www.itstimeto.co.uk